To Trust My Heart

S.L. STERLING

To Trust My Heart

previously titled The Holiday Dilemma

Copyright © 2022 by S.L. Sterling

All rights reserved. Without limiting the rights under copyright reserved about, no part of this publication may be reproduced, stored in, or introduced into a retrieval system, or transmitted in any form or by any means (mechanical, electronic, photocopying, recording, or otherwise) without the prior written permission of both the copyright owner and the above publisher of the book. This is a work of fiction. Any references to historical events, real people, or real places are used fictitiously. Other names, characters, places, and events are products of the author's imagination, and any resemblance to actual events or places or persons, living or dead, is entirely coincidental. Disclaimer: This book contains mature content not suitable for those under the age of 18. It involves strong language and sexual situations. All parties portrayed in sexual situations are consenting adults over the age of 18.

ISBN: 978-1-989566-44-2

Paperback ISBN: 978-1-989566-59-6

Harcover ISBN: 978-1-989566-60-2

Editor: Brandi Aquino, Editing Done Write

Cover Design: Thunderstruck Cover Design

Brooke

THE FIRST SNOWFALL of the season was upon us. Willow Valley had been transformed into a Christmas winter wonderland. The downtown was filled with twinkling lights, red ribbons, and garland and I felt a sense of peace as I looked out the front window of The Crispy Biscuit and watched as more snowflakes danced down to the ground. Christmas was my favorite time of the year. Not only because of how gorgeous Willow Valley became but because I couldn't wait to unleash all the sweet treats I'd decided to add to my bakery counter this year.

"Cinnamon rolls are out of the oven," Melinda called from the kitchen.

"Perfect. As soon as they cool enough to add the new icing drizzle, bring some out here and let's give these ones a try," I said as I looked over the window display I'd just finished. Another perfect setup, I thought to myself as I looked at the twinkling Christmas lights that hung in the window.

This diner was my home away from home. I'd taken over a few years ago, when my parents had been forced to retire. Two years ago, I took over the space of a retired business next door, blew out the wall, and expanded the space. Not only had the expansion created more room, but it had allowed me to put in a separate baking area and large wall ovens specially dedicated for my bakery counter. Not having to share a kitchen with the chef for the diner had allowed me to be able to start baking earlier and at the same time as he was busy cooking breakfast for the diner.

The bakery counter had boomed in the past few years. I'd added more counter space and had gotten a contract from an online retailer, Baking Crate, which allowed me to receive orders and ship my baked goods nationwide.

"Oh and we got another order on Baking Crate dot com, by the way. It just came in—one dozen chocolate donuts."

"Awesome. Please set it aside with the others. I'll get to them tomorrow," I said, pouring two cups of coffee and sliding into the small booth in the back of the now-empty diner.

I'd been working tirelessly on the cinnamon bun recipe for a month now. Every year I baked one brand new item to offer for the holidays. I'd sat down, began creating, and started baking. With each new batch, I tweaked something different, and tonight, after the tenth try, I was sure I'd nailed it. I'd decided to add in a pinch of cinnamon to the icing. I was hoping this was the last change I'd need since, normally, I'd have them in the display case by now.

"Here you go." Melinda carried out two plates, each loaded with a cinnamon roll. "They are still a tad warm, but I think they should be fine that way," she said, placing one of the plates down in front of me and sliding into the booth.

"I sure hope so. It's never taken me this long to create a recipe. It didn't take me this long with the Grinch-A-Mas Cookie, or with the Cocoa Cuddles. I was beginning to feel rather defeated."

"That's because these are going to be a masterpiece." Melinda giggled as she raised her coffee mug. "Not that the others weren't."

"I don't know about that. I mean, I know I won second prize with the Grinch Crinkle Cookies and third with the Joy Givers. I just don't know if these have what it takes to be a bestseller."

"Are you going to enter anything this year?"

"Oh I've thought about it, but with the diner, keeping up with the bakery counter, and all the orders on Baking Crate, I don't know if I have time. I'm probably going to have to hire another person or perhaps two to help us out.

I can't rely on you seven days a week. You need downtime just like I do."

Melinda nodded her head. "You do need downtime." She winked.

I smiled. I'd known we needed help. We needed it back in the summer, and I'd just kind of looked the other way. Melinda had been my right-hand girl for a couple of years, working side-by-side with me, putting in nearly as many hours as I was. She should have been given partial owner-ship, but she never once complained.

"It's not a problem, honestly. I have no one here at all. My father is a Marine and is on another tour. I have no clue where my mother is, and I'm not seeing anyone. Being here with you and the rest of the team fills the void I feel and keeps me out of trouble, especially at Christmas." She smiled.

"Well, I'm glad you're happy. On that note, let's take a bite of these, shall we. See what, if anything, needs to be done to them to make them better."

I sunk my teeth into the soft roll. It had the perfect mix of cinnamon. They were soft, not firm, and they were...perfect.

"My God, Brooke, they taste like heaven!" Melinda exclaimed.

This was it. This was the recipe I'd nearly killed myself over, lost sleep over, and meals, and probably gained close to ten pounds trying. The sweet dessert melted in my mouth. It was the best cinnamon roll I'd ever tasted!

"It must have been the extra dash of cinnamon you added to the icing!" Melinda exclaimed. "These are so good." She shoved another piece into her mouth.

I couldn't help but laugh. "I couldn't agree with you more," I said, taking another bite. I put the bun down and reached for my copy of *Festive Treasures*, my favorite baking magazine. It was their holiday edition, which I loved the most.

"Are they running that contest this year?" Melinda asked as she licked her fingers clean, then grabbed a napkin from the dispenser on the table.

I flipped the magazine open and turned a few pages, "Yep, here it is," I said, reading through the article.

"There's a little more coffee. Did you want a top up?" Melinda asked as I continued reading.

"Yes please."

Melinda slid from the booth, grabbing both mugs, and headed to the coffee pot. I stopped about halfway through and stared down at the magazine. It couldn't be. I blinked hard, wiped at my eyes, and continued reading to make sure I wasn't going crazy. I was concentrating so hard I hadn't noticed Melinda had returned.

"What is it?" she quietly asked.

"It can't be," I muttered.

"What?"

"Um, it says here that they are bringing the contest here, to Willow Valley," I mumbled.

"What! That's so exciting! I mean, that would give you the time to enter, right?"

"There is no way the contest is being held here. They normally host it in New York. It's got to be a mistake."

Melinda reached over and pulled the magazine from me and quickly read the article. "No, it's true. The contest is going to be right here in Willow Valley. You have to enter now!"

I pulled the magazine back and smiled. "I'll think about it. Besides, it's getting late. We should head home. Morning comes early."

"Come on, Brooke, you enter every year. It would be silly not to enter when it's being held in your own back-yard," Melinda said, excitement lining her voice.

I looked up at her and smiled. "Let me think on it."

"Okay." I could hear the disappointment in her voice. "I'll just slip into the kitchen and quickly clean up every-thing and be on my way. You head on home. You started before me."

I nodded. "Thanks, Melinda."

Once I'd grabbed my coat and purse from my office, I left the bakery through the back door and cut across the parking lot to my front door. My house was situated in behind The Crispy Biscuit, it was so nice being so close. I locked my car door before heading inside and made my way to the kitchen to put on dinner.

An hour later I watched Melinda lock up the bakery from my kitchen window as I did the dishes. I was already in my fluffy pajamas, so once I was done, I sat down to try and unwind. I had the first Christmas movie of the season playing on the TV, and I reached for the magazine I'd been reading earlier. The thought of *Festive Treasures* holding their Countdown to Christmas Bake Off event right here in my hometown still blew my mind. I knew I didn't have a choice. I'd have to enter. After all, the past two years in a row, I was the third and second place winner.

I grabbed my laptop and opened it, heading to their website. I figured I'd apply. If I heard back, it would be a bonus. I navigated to the application form and filled it out. When I got to the part of which recipe I was thinking on entering, I stopped and thought for a moment. I'd never entered my Grinch-A-Mas Cookie, or Cocoa Cuddles, yet those cinnamon rolls were on the top of my mind. I hoped that recipe could earn me a first-place ribbon if I were so lucky.

I stared at the screen, hopping between the three recipes, and finally, after much deliberation, I typed in Cinnamon Buns and hit send. There, it was done. I'd entered. I blew out a breath. Melinda was right, they were running the contest here; there was no way I couldn't enter. I navigated away from the page and went to the local job site page and quickly posted a position for some help. If there was any way at all I was going to get through this holiday season, extra help was the key.

It had been a busy morning, the diner had been packed from the time we opened, and we'd had a line out the door for nearly two hours straight this morning with people coming in for coffee and baked goods. Once the line died off, I left Melinda to come into my small office to check email and see if I had any applications. We desperately needed help. There was no doubt about it; this morning had proved it. I opened up my email to find three. The job posting had been up for nearly a week and I'd gotten three applications. I blew out a breath as I opened the first, feeling absolutely defeated as this person had zero experience.

I was halfway through reading over the next person's experience when Melinda came rushing into my office. "Look what just came in!" she said excitedly, as she waved an envelope through the air.

"What is it?" I asked as I watched her and the huge smile on her face.

"It's from *Festive Treasures*," she sang, placing the envelope down in front of me. "Open it!"

I couldn't help but laugh as I picked up the envelope and ripped the end open, sliding the letter out into my hand, quickly reading the first paragraph to myself as Melinda stood there fidgeting about.

"Well? What does it say?"

"We weren't selected as a candidate," I said, lowering my head and folding the letter back up.

"What? What do you mean? How could they? I mean you placed in the top three the last two years, and now they don't want you. What's their address? I will write them. Or better yet, their phone number. I'm going to call them and give them a piece of my mind," Melinda said, pacing back and forth in front of me.

I couldn't help but laugh. "Oh, Melinda, this, this is why I love you! So animated, much like me. You don't need to call or write anyone because we were accepted."

"Oh!"

"Yep," I said, picking the letter back up. "It's with our greatest pleasure to welcome you back to *Festive Treasures* Countdown to Christmas Bake-Off. Please be aware of the following dates: December 1: additional applicant tryouts —you must attend, even though you have been accepted. December 12 is Contest Day, and December 21st, winners will be featured in the *Festive Treasures* magazine. We look forward to meeting you in Willow Valley. Sincerely, Tristan Ryan, Food Critic and Judge Number 3 for this year's Countdown to Christmas Bake-Off."

As Melinda danced around with excitement, I stopped and read over the last part. Tristan Ryan, this year's judge. I was so focused on the name that was written in front of me, I didn't notice Melinda had stopped dancing around and now stood there looking at me with concern.

"Brooke, what is it?" she asked, just as the little bell above the door rang out.

"It's nothing, nothing at all," I said, folding up the paper and shoving it back into the envelope.

"It can't be nothing. You look like you've seen a ghost. Tell me, what is it?"

As she stood there waiting, the bell rang over the door again.

"You better get out there. I need to get through these applications," I gritted.

Melinda looked at me again with concern, then nodded, taking off to the front, and I sat down and pulled the letter out of the envelope. I never thought I'd see his name again, I thought to myself, yet here it was. Could it actually be the same guy I'd gone to culinary school with? He wouldn't be working for some measly little magazine —not with the connections he had. There was no way, I thought to myself, then let out a laugh. He was probably a head chef in some fancy New York restaurant now.

Perhaps even running two or three restaurants and was now up for his second or third Michelin Star by now.

I laughed to myself as I folded the letter back up, shoved it back into the envelope, and pegged it to my cork board. Then I turned to the computer screen and read through the last two applications. Yep, that was it. These were the girls. I printed off their applications and made a mental note to call them later tonight. Then I got up, washed my hands, and got to work baking the cookies and cupcakes for the online orders that had just come in.

Brooke

July 2009

I RAN down the road toward the small coffee shop on the corner. I'd been in the city for two weeks and wanted to get acquainted with the surroundings so that I knew, for the most part, where I was going, instead of having all the pressure of starting a new school in a new location all at once. I'd spent the morning at a yoga class and was now late to meet Emily, my roommate, at the local coffee shop. I pulled the door open and ran inside, only I didn't get very far. Instead, I hit something, flew backward, and landed on the pavement, my water bottle flying from my hand.

"What the hell?" I yelled, as I watched my favorite

purple water bottle fall into the street where it was crushed by an oncoming truck.

"My God. I'm so sorry. I didn't see you. Here, let me help you up," I heard a deep voice say.

I didn't have time to protest because before I knew it, I was already standing on both of my feet looking into the face of an extremely handsome man.

"Thank you," I muttered as I brushed myself off, somewhat embarrassed at the fact I'd literally run into him.

"Good thing I decided to stay and have my coffee. This could have turned out to be much worse than it is." He chuckled, his blue eyes sparkling. "You sure you're all right?" he questioned, bending to meet my eyes.

I nodded. "Just got the wind knocked out of me," I mumbled, just as the door to the coffee shop opened and Emily came rushing out. "My goodness are you all right?" she said, rushing to my side.

"I'm fine," I mumbled, looking into the face of the tall blond-haired, blue-eyed man. He was gorgeous, and I could feel the butterflies in my stomach at the fact he'd had his hands on me, even if it was only to help me up. "I was rushing because I was late," I whispered to Emily.

"You should be more careful next time," the man across from me blurted out as if I had been talking to him.

"Excuse me?" I bit out. "I was speaking to my friend. And why should I be more careful?"

"Well, running into doors where people on the other side could be walking out of carrying hot liquid isn't that smart, so, yes you should be more careful."

"Perhaps you should be the one who is more careful and check to see that someone isn't running inside before walking out of said door. Did you ever think of that?" I said defensively.

"Whoa, you guys, it was an accident. Surely, neither one of you meant to run into one another." Emily giggled.

Emily was right, this was ridiculous, fighting over something so silly as whose fault it was to run into one another. As Emily laughed, I could feel the twitch in my lip start, and soon I too began laughing, then so did the gorgeous man in front of me. People were beginning to look at us as we all stood there laughing.

"What's your name?" he questioned.

"Lila," I lied, giving him my mother's name, which did happen to be my middle name. Emily looked at me with a frown.

"Well, Lila, it was nice to meet you. Hope to run into you again some time." He winked. "Not in the literal sense though, but perhaps we could have a coffee date sometime," he said, reaching into his pocket and pulling out a card, holding it out for me to take.

When I didn't immediately take the card, Emily reached out and grabbed it. "Thank you." She shoved the card into my hand as he smiled at me. "She'll call you."

"I look forward to it," he said, his eyes washing over my body. He smiled, then turned and walked down the road in the direction I'd come from.

"What the hell was that? Your name isn't Lila." Emily said as soon as he was out of earshot, shocked at the fact I'd lied.

I shrugged. "Mama told me not to give my real name out to complete strangers, but it wasn't a full-on lie. It is my middle name. Besides, it's not like I'll ever see him again," I said, throwing the card into the garbage.

"What are you doing?" Emily squealed, practically diving into the garbage after the card and rescuing it.

"I'm not going to call, nor have coffee with him, so there is no need to keep the card." I shrugged.

"His name is Tristan...and he's..."

I held my hand out, stopping her from reading any further. "Please...I don't care. Now let's go and have our coffee." I smiled and carefully pulled the door open and stepped inside.

As the last few weeks of summer rolled on, I knew school would be starting. I'd gone shopping for some school supplies and hopped off the bus and swung my book bag over my shoulder. I glanced at my watch. I still had a few hours to kill before I had to be anywhere. Plenty of time to grab a coffee and perhaps a snack, I thought to myself, realizing I'd not eaten all day. I pulled open the door to the same coffee shop Emily and I had visited, this time careful to check and make sure no one was coming out. I hadn't been back there since I'd run into the handsome stranger.

I stepped inside and took a deep breath, the smell of freshly brewed coffee hitting me. It had been my favorite smell since I'd been a small child, helping my mom on the weekends at The Crispy Biscuit. I stepped up to the counter and waited, while the girl dumped a fresh pot of water into the coffeemaker.

"Can I help you?"

"I'll have a large coffee, two sugars, one cream please," I said, reaching into my pocket and pulling out some money. "And a blueberry muffin," I added, eying the large muffins in the display case.

"Well, here she is. She shows up again, but sadly never called," I heard a deep voice from behind me say.

I turned abruptly and came face-to-face with the gorgeous man I'd run into only a few weeks earlier. I softly smiled. "I misplaced your number," I lied.

"You probably threw it away, like most women I meet." He laughed, then winked. "Care to join me for a bite. I have about an hour or so before I have to be anywhere."

I met his eyes, not answering him. Did women really do that? Throw away his number the instant they got it. There was no way I could believe that. He seemed far too nice for them to do that.

"Lila? Wasn't it?" he asked. "You don't have to, if you'd prefer not to."

I nodded. "No, I think that would be nice," I answered just as the girl placed my coffee and muffin on the counter.

"That will be five fifty," she said.

"Here, let me. Add my order as well, thanks," he said, removing his wallet from his back pocket and pulling out a twenty.

The girl behind the counter met my eyes and softly smiled. I picked my coffee up and made my way over to a small table in the corner and sat down, while he ordered. Then I watched as he too carried his order over and took a seat across from me.

The conversation flowed easily. We spoke of nothing personal at first. In fact, I still didn't even know his full name, and he still thought mine was Lila. It was funny how I'd gotten lost in his eyes and his voice, and soon the conversation shifted from casual to personal. I thought nothing of it and sat there answering his questions, until he asked the one that made my stomach tingle.

"So, Lila, are you seeing anyone?" he asked with curiosity and a hint of hope in his eyes.

I didn't know why the question surprised me. I had seen the way he'd been looking at me for the past half hour. Yet I sat there shocked, shaking my head. "No, I'm single. What about you?" I questioned, swallowing hard.

He shrugged. "Not really. I just arrived in this city two months ago. Haven't really had too much time to meet anyone," he answered, glancing at his watch.

I too glanced at mine and realized I was late for my yoga class. "Shit," I muttered under my breath.

"What is it?"

"I'm late. I was supposed to meet my friend for yoga class." I shrugged.

"Just so happens I'm late as well," he said, crumpling his muffin wrapper in his large, strong hands.

He smiled, and suddenly I'd wished I'd told him my real name, but now it was too late. I'd just have to leave it. It wasn't as if I'd planned on seeing him again.

"Well, Lila, thank you for the company. I hope to see you around sometime. Would it be okay if I called you sometime?" he questioned sliding out of his chair and standing.

"Sure, I guess," I said, sliding out of the seat this time. He placed his business card down on the table and pulled a pen from his suit jacket. I quickly scribbled down my cell number and handed him back his pen. This time, unlike the last, he didn't leave me his card. Instead, he picked up the one I'd put my number on and winked as he shoved it into his pocket. "I'll call you," he said, giving me that sexy smile, then placing his hand on my lower back he guided me to the door

.

Four weeks later, I stood outside of the school and looked up at the huge sign that hung across the front of the main building. I was beyond excited to be here and to be starting my first day of class. Tasty Temptations was one of the top cooking schools, and since I had enjoyed and passed a few cooking courses in the spring at a small school in Willow Valley, I'd decided to come here and complete their pastry course. If all went well and I liked it here, I would proceed with their culinary course.

I walked up the steps and into the main building and found Room 249 and pulled the door open to find the class was just about full. The instructor sat behind her desk going over what I assumed were her notes for the day. She glanced my way, smiled, and then stood.

"Looks like we are all here now. Welcome. Everyone please take a seat. We are going to take a few minutes, go around the room, and introduce ourselves. I'll start first. My name is Evangeline. I have twenty-five years' experience teaching others how to make world class pastries. I've traveled and studied pastries all over the world. I've trained in some of the best restaurants in Paris, Italy, Texas, and Hawaii, just to name a few."

She was about to go on when the door flew open. I

glanced over and immediately buried my face in my hands. It was the guy from the coffee shop. After the morning I'd given him my number, he had called a couple of times, perhaps three; however, both times I was occupied and unable to get to my phone. The calls had stopped after that.

"Sorry I'm late. Took forever to get across campus. You can carry on now." He chuckled, looking around the room.

Evangeline just stared, probably unsure what to say, and I rolled my eyes. How rude of him to be like that, I thought. I looked in his direction, and that was when he made eye contact with me. I could tell he recognized me right away. Evangeline just stood there, staring at him with a frown on her face. She seemed to be at a loss for words at the way he'd interrupted without a care.

"Next time you're late, you'll care to knock first before you barge in here and interrupt me. Do I make myself clear, Mr. Uh.... Mr...."

"Ryan, Tristan Ryan."

"Mr. Ryan, take a seat, would you."

I was still staring at him, disgusted with the way he'd interrupted the class. He glanced around the room, and that was when I noticed there were only two empty seats available. One at an empty table and the one beside me.

I practically shouted out loud for him to sit at the other table, but thankfully, I only said it in my head. I looked down at where my hands were crossed on the tabletop in front of me, praying he took the other empty seat. When I glanced over again, he looked directly at me, walked across the room, and slid in beside me, placing his arm across the back of the bench.

"Well, if it isn't the girl from the coffee shop." He leaned over and whispered in my ear, "The very one who never returned my calls. Hello, Lila."

He smelled so good, and the sound of his voice caused a chill to run through me. I never should have given him a fake name. In a few short minutes, he would know who I really was—a total liar—and I already wanted to die of embarrassment. I couldn't use a fake name here.

The instructor moved on as if nothing had happened, going around the room to each student so they could introduce themselves. I listened, fascinated as I heard some of the accomplishments from some of them. Then Evangeline set eyes on me.

"You must be Brooke Kinley. Why don't you tell us about yourself," she said as she leaned against her desk.

I looked up and glanced around the room. Everyone had their eyes on me, including Tristan. I tried to avoid meeting his eyes, but it was impossible. He looked shocked, and I felt as if I were on fire. I swallowed hard and smiled nervously, feeling as if everyone knew me as Lila.

"Tsk tsk tsk," I heard him whisper. "You lied to me about your name," he said, staring up at me.

I swallowed hard, my stomach full of butterflies as the class looked at me. "I'm Brooke Kinley. I'm here to complete the pastry chef program and plan to continue on to the culinary once that is completed. I moved here from the small town of Willow Valley. My parents own a small diner there, and since it's been in the family for generations, my parents would like to see me take it over once they retire. It's always been my dream to open a small bakery, and I hope to be able to add that aspect of the business to the small diner once I return."

"Whoa, wait a minute," Tristan said, interrupting me.

I glanced to Evangeline, who crossed her arms in front of her chest and leaned up against the desk, waiting for Tristan to speak.

"You've come to take a culinary course and pastry chef program to waste the talents you learn here in some small-town diner?" He laughed.

"Excuse me?" I bit out.

"Well, I mean, I'm sure you know how to bake and cook. That should be good enough for the small-town diner. I mean, most of those types of people won't even have a clue what cronut or a zeppoli is. In my opinion, you're wasting your time and money."

I looked around the class as all eyes were on me. Some sat with a smile, others were shocked. Was he doing this over the name thing, I wondered? I sucked in a deep breath, and even though my stomach was now swirling, I swallowed hard and did my best to keep my composure. "That's your opinion."

"It should be yours too. You're wasting your money here if you don't plan to go to New York or to Paris. It's completely pointless."

At his words, somewhere inside of me a fire was brewing. "Oh let me guess. I'm just some small-town hick who should learn how to bake in my grandmother's kitchen, is that correct?" I said, holding my head high. There was no way I was going to let this cocky, arrogant jerk get away with putting me down, and in that moment, I was glad that I'd never called him back or told him much about myself.

"If the shoe fits, Lila."

There it was, and there was that grin. The same grin he interrupted the instructor with when he'd come through the door, and the same grin he'd given me when we ran into one another out front of the coffee shop.

Every fiber of my body was on alert, and I couldn't clench my fists any tighter.

"Well, it so happens that as it stands right now, I could probably bake you right underneath this table. You may happen to know names of fancy pastries, but you've probably only ever ate them. You've probably never had to make them."

He chuckled. "What's your point?"

"My point is that it's entirely different. It actually takes some sort of skill to make them. It doesn't take any skill to shove them in your face and chew." The class erupted into laughter at my rebuttal, but Evangeline quickly quieted down the class.

"Mr. Ryan, why don't you tell us what you're doing here?" she said, crossing her arms in front of her.

"Well, I'm from New York. I grew up in some of the finest and fanciest restaurants around the world. Cooking has always been a passion of mine, and once I graduate, I want to open up my own restaurant. I plan to be a four-star Michelin chef by the time I hit thirty."

I couldn't help but burst into laughter. "Are you freaking kidding us right now." I laughed. "A four-star Michelin chef by the time you're thirty."

"What? Are you saying it can't be done?" he said, turning those bright-blue eyes on me.

How had I found them attractive before, I wondered.

"You're going to become a four-star Michelin chef?" I said, looking him over. "By the time you're thirty, doing a pastry program."

"I'm also taking the culinary program at the same time. That way I don't waste my time spreading it out over the four years."

"Yeah, okay, good luck with that." I laughed.

"What's that supposed to mean?" he questioned.

"It means that you should be devoting your time to one, not both at the same time. They take dedication and focus, so as I said, good luck with that."

"Look, it may be hard for some chick who hails from.... what valley did you say?"

"All right, that's enough, the two of you," Evangeline demanded. "I will not have my students ripping up one another's dreams, whatever they may be. Now since we've had both your introductions, and you were the last two, I guess we will start the class..."

I watched as Tristan turned to face Evangeline. There was no way I was going to make it through the next two years if this guy was sitting beside me every single day. He would probably do all he could to sabotage me. Regardless, I pulled my pencil from my bag and opened my notebook and began taking notes. I'd talk to Evangeline after class if I had to.

It was all I could do to keep my mouth shut the remainder of the class. Every time Tristan opened his mouth, I wanted to scream. He was so arrogant, such a know-it-all. In fact, the instructor had to correct him more times than any of us. Such a different guy from the one I'd met in the coffee shop.

Tristan

THE FIRST THREE months of classes had gone by in a flash. It had been mostly note taking, but tomorrow was our first hands-on assignment. Brooke and I had to make a red velvet cake with a cream cheese frosting. I was the one who had pulled the card out of the basket, and when I read it aloud, she'd looked at me with worry in her eyes.

She leaned over and whispered in my ear, "Can you bake?"

I could hear her voice in my head as I laid in my bed in my dorm room, staring up at the ceiling. My computer sat open on the small desk in my room, the fan humming away as I remembered the twinkle in her deep-blue eyes. I'd spent most of my nights in this same position, thinking about Brooke every single night.

I found her so attractive, and I wanted to get closer to

her. I still didn't know why she'd lied to me about her name. I guessed I'd never know, but whatever her reason I was sure it was a good one. Still, walking into that classroom on the first day, seeing her there, had knocked the wind out of me when my eyes landed on hers. As usual, I was an ass, and I'd treated her like shit. However, the more time I spent with her, the more beautiful she was becoming to me, and I wanted to find some way for her to notice me as more than just an arrogant ass. Yet every single day was the same. I couldn't turn off that side of me.

I'd continued being that arrogant prick to her, just like my brother said I was to every girl I'd ever liked. I'd practically given her shit for running into me the first time we ran into one another, and then the first day of class I'd made fun of her, as I'd done each day thereafter. The only time I'd been normal had been the morning we ran into one another and shared a coffee together. I shook my head. There was no way any girl in her right mind would date me after I acted like that. Which was exactly why I was still single.

I sat up and reached for my phone, dialing my older brother, Zach. He'd know what to do. After all, he'd been married now for almost five years. I'd always gone to him for advice, normally when it was too late, which perhaps this time I had some room to make it up. At least I hoped I still had time.

"Hello," he answered. I could tell from the noise in the background he was driving.

"Zach, it's Tristan."

"Hey, man, how's it going? How is school?"

"Good, good."

"What's up, what do you need?" he asked.

"Do you have a second? I mean, I can tell you are driving."

"Yep, it's fine. I'm just about to drop Lana off. Give me two seconds to pull over."

I waited for a couple of minutes and finally heard my brother's voice. "Okay, I'm waiting here, so dump on me."

"Well, I met someone."

"Oh, do tell," Zach said. I imagined him rubbing his hands together, getting ready to dump all of his worldly love advice onto me. "What's her name?"

"Lil—" I stopped myself. "Brooke."

"Lil Brooke?" Zach questioned. "What kind of a name is that?"

"No, no, just Brooke," I said.

"Okay."

"Well, you see, I met her at a coffee shop. She was running into the place, while I was leaving, and we literally collided."

"Was she all right?"

Okay, so I got two points, I thought to myself. I'd asked her if she was all right. "Yes, she was fine."

"Okay, and what happened next? You helped her up I hope."

"I did." Another two points, I thought to myself. "However, that is when it turned bad."

"Uh-huh."

"It's just she was so beautiful, and well, me and my big mouth chided her for not being more careful."

"Oh no." I heard Zach blow out a breath and imagined he was pinching the bridge of his nose with his fingers, just as he always did when I brought him girl issues.

"Yep, but it gets better."

"Oh I bet."

"Two weeks later, I ran into her again at the coffee shop. We shared a coffee, just casual talk, and then we had to part ways. I got her to give me her number, and I tried calling, but she was never there. I'd given up, but then I ran into her again because she's in the same pastry course and is now my partner for the semester."

Zach chuckled. "I see. How did that happen?"

"Well, I was late for class, and when I arrived, she had the only open seat next to her, so I took it. Then she proceeded to tell the class all about why she was there."

"Let me guess, you brought fourth your usual cockiness and put her down, and then proceeded to show her what a truly arrogant ass you can be and went on about the Michelin chef thing, am I right."

My brother knew me well. Way too well at times. We'd both been raised by affluent parents. We'd wanted for nothing. Yet it was as if Zach and I had each grown up in different homes. He'd worked hard for everything he had, never taking the handouts our parents could offer. In many ways, I knew that had made him a much better person than me. I had done the opposite, and many times had been told by my brother that I was nothing but a spoiled, stuck-up brat.

"Yep."

"Why do you do that?" Zach questioned. "Why do you put people down, or have to show them up?"

"I don't know. I just can't stand when someone doesn't want to better themselves and then go after all they could get."

Zach laughed. "Wait a minute. Who is this and where the hell did Tristan go?" He chuckled. "You don't like it if someone doesn't want to better themselves?" He laughed. "Who the hell are you? If you have your way, you'll complete this course, and then Dad will work his magic and make sure you get the status you want by paying someone off. That isn't working hard and going after all you could get. It's bribery, plain and simple. How about you try something new and put some effort into it and work for something, just for once, and make it happen entirely all on your own."

"I am working on making it happen. Dad says he

won't do anything unless I pass these courses. Do you have any idea how hard this is going to be?"

"Why, because he isn't going to pay off the teacher to get you a passing mark? Besides, that's not what I mean, and you know it. Now what is it that this girl said that made you get all wound up?"

"Well, instead of going off to New York or some other huge city and putting her education to use, all she is planning on using it for is to work in some crappy small-town diner that her parents own."

The line was silent for a moment. Then I heard Zach sigh. "Perhaps that is what makes her happy? Did you think of that? Perhaps that is success to her?"

"Ummm…" I paused, trying to wrap my head around what he was saying. I had never thought of that, but I also couldn't see how that could be defined as success either.

"You didn't, did you? Tristan, you say you like this girl?" Zach asked.

"Yeah, she's a cutie."

"Well, perhaps you should talk less and listen more. Actually hear what it is she is saying instead of just analyzing the surface. Get to know her, and not just the outer part of her. You can be the most attractive person in the world, but if the personality doesn't match, well…"

My brother had never spoken to me like that before. I thought about what had happened today and over the past three months and realized that perhaps he was right. Perhaps I didn't listen to what it was she was saying.

"I suppose you might be right."

"You know, not everyone has to be the same as you. If you were actually going to work for what you wanted, you might understand that. You might understand the dedication and hard work it takes to build something. You might also understand what I mean when I say success isn't the same for everyone. But when I know for a fact that you hand Dad a good grade, he is going to slide you into one of the top restaurants in New York for a job, and then he's going to bribe someone to give you what you want, it makes me sick to my stomach."

I listened to my brother. Most of what he was saying was making me angry, but I was trying. Zach had worked his way up in the company he worked for. He had started in the mail room and had risen right through the ranks and now was one of the three CEOs of the company. He had done it all on his own and never once complained. He had never once quit when things got hard, and he'd never once refused to do something. It was amazing how differently we turned out coming from the same family.

"Tristen, you can do whatever you'd like to try and get this girl, but I say, talk less, listen more, and maybe you should work for something, for yourself, instead of just taking the easy way out."

"Thanks, Zach," I said, rolling my eyes at his advice.

"Look, I've got to go. Lana is back. We're headed out for dinner. Just try what I say."

"Okay, have fun."

I hung up the phone and flopped back down on the bed. Was Zach right? Had I really done this all my life? Had I really only ever taken handouts from Mom and Dad?

I was already seated in class the next morning, flipping through the textbook, when Brooke walked in. She was smiling and laughing with two of the other girls when she looked up and met my eyes. Instantly, the smile was washed from her face as she approached our instructor and whispered something to her.

I watched the exchange between them. Brooke said something, the instructor shook her head, Brooke rebutted, the instructor once again shook her head. She went to say something else, but the instructor turned away from her. Then, with her head down, she made her way over to the seat beside mine and slipped in without so much as a word.

"Good morning," I said, leaning over to her, and in the process catching a whiff of her perfume.

"Is it?" she questioned, opening her books.

"Looks like it." I chuckled. When she didn't laugh, I shifted uncomfortably in my seat. "Look, I think perhaps we may have gotten off on the wrong foot."

"Is that so?" she said while flipping through the pages of her book.

"Yes."

"Hmm, imagine that."

"Think we could start over?"

Brooke sat there, not saying anything, just flipping through her textbook page by page. "I don't know. Depends on you."

"Okay, well, first let me apologize for everything. How I've been acting was uncalled for."

Brooke looked over at me and squinted her eyes.

"I shouldn't have been so judgmental. I am sure that you have your reasons for being here."

"I do, thank you. As I'm sure you have yours."

I nodded. "Yes, and if you feel you need to know how to make fine little deserts when scones and butter tarts would probably do, then more power to you."

She stopped thumbing through her textbook and looked at me. "What is that supposed to mean?"

"Well, you say you live in a small town. I've never heard of Willow Valley. In fact, I don't even have a clue where it is, but I am sure most of the people who live there have never set foot outside of it. They probably all love seasonal pies and cookies and have never truly had a wonderful desert like they serve in the big cities. So, as I said, if you want to waste your time when scones and butter tarts would do, go for it."

Brooke looked at me, a frown on her face, and turned back to her book. Slowly flipping the pages. "You know, I was going to give you the benefit of the doubt, but I think that has passed. So, how about we don't speak anymore. Oh, and I tried to get you a new partner, however Evangeline said no. So, let's just work through this year, and next year we can separate."

I was about to say something when Evangeline stood up and began speaking. I stared at Brooke for a moment, watching as she began making notes, and when she didn't look back at me, I turned my attention to the instructor. I'd had one task—just shut up and listen—and I'd been incapable of doing that.

Brooke

1 year later

I MADE my way into the small coffee shop on campus. It was quieter than usual this morning, but then I realized that most of the classes had already had their finals, and most students had gone home for the summer. I placed my order and then took my coffee and croissant to a small table in the corner.

My stomach turned as I spread a little jam onto the pastry and took a bite. Today was the only day that truly mattered, I thought to myself. The final challenge of the year, the final exam. It was a two-part exam, half written and the other practical. I took a sip of my coffee and swallowed the hot liquid. I was nervous, and my hand shook as I set the cup back down on the table.

It wasn't the doubt in my ability that was making me shake, but the scene that I figured would arise during the final exam. Every week this past year we'd had a challenge, and I'd passed every one of them with zero help from Tristan. In fact, I'd have failed every single joint challenge had I not taken charge and told him to sit there and be quiet. Had I not done that, I feared each joint challenge would have ended up like his independent challenges. It wasn't that he'd received a failing mark, especially once he began copying each step as I did them, but each were marked with a "needs improvement."

However, in the end, we both ended up with a passing grade going into the exam. I wasn't sure if he had stayed behind in class to make up extra grades or what, but by my calculations, and what I'd seen, he should have been failing. I was shocked when our grades were posted yesterday, and I saw where he was sitting. I was at ninety-five and he was at ninety-three.

I took another bite of my croissant. Our final exam today was worth fifty percent of our mark, and I feared what would happen if, in fact, we were paired up. I glanced down at my watch and noticed I had twenty minutes to get across campus and into the class. I shoved the last of my breakfast in my face, grabbed my book bag and coffee, and made a dash for the door.

I sat in the classroom, beside Tristan, trying to listen to what Evangeline was saying. He was gazing out the window, like he usually did, not paying attention to anything, only this time he was tapping his pencil on the desk. The constant drumming was driving me crazy, and I reached across and ripped the pencil from his hand. His head spun around and his eyes locked with mine for a second, but I focused my attention on Evangeline.

"For the practical component of the final exam this year, we will be making French macarons. You can work together or apart but let me remind you that if you should choose to work together, you will be graded together," Evangeline said.

I watched as she made her way to the back of the class and turned the lights on over the baking area. There were enough spaces for each one of us in the class to work alone, yet some of the pairs were already joining together, like I knew they would. I went to get up and make my way to the back when I felt Tristan grab my wrist.

"Brooke, can I talk to you for a second?" he questioned.

I let out a breath, annoyed at the fact that he'd stopped me, "What is it?" I asked.

"Can we work together on this one?"

I couldn't help but laugh. Why on earth would he even think I'd consider working with him on this? It was the final mark of the year, and if this went the same as all the other projects we'd worked on, well, I'd fail. I shook my head. "I don't think that would be wise."

"But, Brooke, I…"

"No, Tristan. I wish you luck, but I am working by myself," I said and made my way back to the back of the room.

Tristan must have followed closely behind me because he slid into the small workspace across from mine, just like he normally did. He looked around nervously, as if he had no clue what he was doing.

"Class, you have two hours… Get to work," Evangeline said. "Those of you working together, please keep the talking to a minimum so you don't disrupt the others."

I took a minute and got myself adjusted, placing my bowls where I wanted them, then I got to work creating my filling. I wanted to make sure I got my idea for the filling down on paper before I began making anything. I quickly marked down the recipe from my grandmother on a piece of paper from memory—a whipped chocolate and coconut ganache that had been my favorite filling growing up. I doubted anyone would have anything like it.

Once I was satisfied, I grabbed the sifter from under the counter and a bowl and began filling the sifter with icing sugar. Once I'd sifted that, I poured the ground almonds into the sifter and sifted that into the icing sugar. I reached under the counter and pulled out a second bowl, dumping the sifted contents back into the sifter and starting again.

"What are you doing?" Tristan asked, looking over at me.

I didn't answer. I just kept sifting away.

"Seriously, how many times are you going to sift that?" he asked, already pulling out the blender.

Again, I ignored him, grabbing the food processor and plugging it in before dumping the mix of icing sugar and ground almonds into it. I turned it on, allowing the mixture to spin around the machine then dumping it back into the sifter. I went about this process three more times and then looked over at Tristan, who stood there smirking.

"What?" I mouthed.

"Bit much don't you think? Wasting all this time sifting that?"

"Whatever you say." I knew from what I'd read that was the secret.

"Mr. Ryan and Miss. Kinley, if you wanted to work together you should have. That's enough talking. Get back to work," Evangeline said, coming up and checking on us both.

I set aside the mixture and grabbed the bowl of egg whites and cream of tartar. I turned on the mixer and began whipping the egg whites, slowly adding in the cream of tartar as soon as the egg whites began to foam, and then began slowly adding in granulated sugar. I tipped in some purple food coloring and continued beating until stiff peaks began forming and softly smiled to myself. Everything was coming together just the way it should.

I glanced over at Tristan. His hair was disheveled and he looked puzzled. He appeared to be having trouble with the egg whites as he looked over to see mine. He then put his head down and continued trying to get his to look the same as mine, but I knew he had added in the cream of tartar too fast and was certain his machine wasn't on a high enough setting. It was impossible that they'd turn out because they weren't being beaten fast enough for them to form.

I slowly began folding in the sugar and ground almonds, carefully folding the already stiffened egg whites and dry ingredients all together. I was completely pleased with the way they were turning out, and once I was happy with the consistency, I did my drop test. Sure enough, the lava-like dough dropped a figure eight perfectly without breaking, and so I began to fill my piping bag, carefully piping uniform drops on the baking sheet in front of me.

When I was finished, I looked over to the mess Tristan had in front of him. His dough was a runny mess and he looked completely frustrated. In that moment, for some reason, I felt bad for him. I didn't know why it was I felt bad for him, to be honest. He'd never cared for anyone else, but in some weird way, as I watched him struggling, I felt bad for him.

I turned my attention back to my tray and gently tapped it on the counter, releasing any air bubbles from the dough, and then set it aside. Then I turned my attention to the filling. It would easily take me forty minutes to get that part of the recipe done, so I focused all my attention to that.

The afternoon passed fairly quickly, and before I knew it. my French macarons sat in front of me on the plate. I was so proud of the way they'd turned out and was even more pleased when Evangeline looked at my plate and picked one of them up, taking a bite.

"Very good, Brooke. These are amazing," she said, smiling at me, "That filling is superb.

She said nothing more, then walked over to Tristan, whose macarons looked nothing like mine. She did the same thing, looking them over and taking a small bite, only she said nothing, but the raised eyebrow gave me an indication of how he'd done.

"Congratulations, class. Marks will be posted by next week. You may take what you baked with you should you want. You may start cleanup now, then once you are finished, you may head to your seats and begin the written portion of the exam."

I glanced over to Tristan whose workspace was still a disaster. I had already cleaned mine up, since I had been finished early enough. I grabbed a small container from my bag and carefully placed my macarons inside. Then I washed up the plate they'd been sitting on, wiped down the counter, and made my way back to my desk where I began working on the last portion of the exam.

I stood outside of the classroom and looked at the marks posted. I ran my finger down the list when I heard someone clear their throat behind me.

"I don't know why you're even checking. You know you passed," the familiar voice said.

"I wanted to see if for myself," I bit out, running my finger down the list to find my name and beside it I saw a mark of ninety-six. I couldn't help but feel amazed as I blinked, only to see the mark again.

Then I saw his hand on the paper and could feel the heat from his body behind me as he ran his finger down the list. I couldn't help but follow it and was shocked to see he had a sixty-five. How badly did he fail that last exam, I wondered.

"You passed as well," I said, my voice full of shock, then I cleared my throat.

"Did you have any doubt?" he asked.

I didn't know what to say. To me, that mark was nothing to be proud of. I turned and met his eyes.

"Well, I guess I will see you next year?" he said, leaning up against the wall. "Have a good summer."

"Yep, you too. I look forward to being neck in neck with you all year. Well, until the final exam that is." I smirked. "I have to catch my bus," I said, picking up my bag off the floor.

"Where are you going?" he questioned, looking at the bags.

"Home for a couple of weeks. What about you?"

"I'm heading home as well. I'll be gone most of the summer, but I'll see you in the fall."

"Sounds good. Have a safe trip," I said, picking up the rest of my bags.

"You too."

I spent the summer back home in Willow Valley. I helped my parents with the diner, spent time with friends, and spent my weekends practicing my pastries. I wanted to be prepared for next year. Two weeks before I was supposed to return to school I'd received a text message from Tristan. I was shocked and surprised at the same time, so much so that I'd decided to text Emily instead of responding to Tristan. After I'd asked her what I should say, I replied with asking him how he was. Only, to my surprise, he never responded.

Before long I was back at the dorms and beginning the first day of class. I'd wandered into the assigned home room and took a seat. I watched with some funny sort of anticipation building as each student entered the room. As the classroom filled up, that anticipation sank, and soon the instructor stood in front of the class, giving his introduction speech.

I never laid eyes on Tristan Ryan again.

Brooke

Present Day - December

Snow was falling heavily outside, accumulating faster than the roads could be cleared. It had started off as a busy morning, but as the storm grew, it became quiet. I'd told Melinda she could have the rest of the day off if she wanted and so she took off. After she left, I'd gone back into the kitchen and pulled the chocolate chip cookies I'd been baking out of the oven when I heard the door chimes go.

I went back out into the front and was surprised to see Trinity and Peggy standing just inside the door, both of them covered in snow, laughing as they brushed themselves off.

"Ladies, come in. I didn't think you'd be coming today," I said as they both took their coats off.

"Better late than never," Trinity said, slipping out of her coat. "I hope you have a pot of coffee on."

"Do I have coffee on? Has the Crispy Biscuit ever let you down?" I giggled, pulling two cups off the cup stand. "Did you ladies want anything to eat?" I asked.

"Did you ever get those cinnamon buns done?" Peggy asked, slipping into their usual booth.

"I did. As a matter of fact, I just made them fresh this morning. You'll have to let me know what you think of them," I said as I plated one for each of them and set them on the tray with their coffees and made my way over to the table.

I placed both coffees in front of them and then placed the plates down on the table. "Enjoy, ladies. Let me know what you think of those."

"Oh my gosh, Brooke, these mugs are adorable!" Trinity said, picking hers up and looking at it.

I'd ordered in custom holiday mugs for this holiday season and they'd arrived yesterday. "Thanks, there are four different ones, I figured they were a nice touch to add to the festive holiday feel around here."

"They are just absolutely adorable!" Peggy said, looking at hers and smiling.

"Glad you like them, today is the first day I've had them out. I was hoping that Thomas would have had my new cupboard completed, but he let me know he was running a bit behind on it.

"Yes, it should be here in the next couple of weeks. He does send his apologies."

"No worries. Enjoy, ladies." I smiled before leaving them to enjoy the cinnamon roll and went into the office and sat down behind the desk and opened my email. Immediately, my eyes landed on the email I'd been avoiding most of the week.

Festive Treasures had been waiting to hear from me, to know what recipe they could be expecting. I opened the email and read it over for the sixth time, hoping that perhaps the wording had changed and that they were going to kick me out of the contest instead. However, the words hadn't changed.

I looked at the deadline date, I had to let them know by tomorrow or else they would disqualify me from the contest. I pulled the letter off the peg board and opened it, reading over the acceptance once again. Then I stared down at the name that was signed on the bottom.

I'd had no idea what had happened to Tristan. I remembered I'd asked around at school, but no one knew much of anything. In fact, most students wondered why I even cared after all the trouble he'd been during the first year. I'd even eventually broken down and tried messaging him again, but it did little good; it was as if he had disappeared off the earth. Until now. As I sat there, I silently wondered if he'd ever gotten his Michelin Stars that he'd wanted so badly back in the day and I giggled to myself. I opened my browser and googled his name, nothing about Michelin Stars came up, just a bunch of articles he'd written over the years with *Festive Treasures* populated the screen and a Facebook profile. As I scrolled, I noticed one of the most recent articles: a congratulatory post, congratulating him on becoming a judge for this year's Countdown to Christmas.

As I read the words, a sinking feeling came over me. Was he really going to be one of the judges for the contest this year? There was no way this was happening! Looked like out of the both of us, I had become the more successful one, I thought, thinking back to how he'd made fun of me that first day. As I ran over the memory in my mind, I decided that there was no way I wasn't going to enter this contest. I was a damn good baker and chef and I planned to win this contest this year, and I feared with him as one of the judges, he would let it get too personal. I folded the letter up and pegged it back up on my board and then hit reply to that email.

In a matter of minutes, I sat reading what I'd written, thanking them for the opportunity but that I would not be participating in this year's contest. I stared at the screen, my mouse hovering over the send button, every fiber of my being screaming back at me. Why the hell shouldn't I participate? Surely, after all these years, he wouldn't still be so cocky. There was no way possible I would have a mark on my back. He probably didn't even remember me, and there were other judges judging this year's contest. He wasn't the final say. I blew out a breath, and instead of hitting send, I deleted all the words I had written and began again, this time letting them know I was delighted to be participating and that I'd be entering my cinnamon rolls.

I hit sent without giving it a second thought, and then I stepped out front to find Trinity and Peggy still laughing away, their plates clean. "So, ladies, how was that cinnamon bun?"

"Fantastic," they said in unison.

"Best I've ever had," Trinity answered. "I'll have to get some to-go. Thomas will love them. I'll also have to take some out to Aunt Vi and Jed when we visit next week."

I smiled. "You got it. Oh, not sure if you heard yet, but I was accepted into the *Festive Treasures* Countdown to Christmas Bake-Off again this year. That is the recipe I have decided to enter."

"Oh, I just got that magazine in the mail," Peggy said. "I haven't read anything about this contest though."

"I've entered before. They've held it for the last couple of years. But this year they are holding it right here in Willow Valley."

"Oh wow. How did we get so lucky?" Trinity questioned.

"I'm not sure. I was the second-place winner last year. Perhaps that is how," I replied, thinking back to the location of last year's contest. They had held it in the winner's hometown though, not the runner-up.

"I hope you ladies will come and root me on. Perhaps even enter into the contest as well," I said, tapping Trinity on the shoulder. "They are having additional tryouts on the first."

"Ha, no way. My baking can't hold a candle to yours." Trinity laughed.

"What about you, Peggy?" I questioned.

"If it were flower arranging, I'd enter in a moment, but baking, you know as well as I do that I purchase all my baking here."

"Well, I tried." I shrugged. "Care for another coffee, ladies?" I asked, looking down at their empty mugs.

They both nodded. I made my way behind the counter and had just picked up the coffee pot when the door opened and Melinda walked in.

"What are you doing here? I thought I gave you the day off?" I giggled, coming around and refilling both mugs.

"You did. I got my errands done and was bored. So, I figured I'd come back in and help you get caught up on those Baking Crate orders."

"I appreciate it. You know I can always use the help for those." I smiled.

Trinity and Peggy had left shortly after three, each with a box of cinnamon buns. I looked out onto the street after they left; it was empty, so I turned the open sign off. The snow was really coming down now, to the point I could barely see across the street, and I hadn't seen anyone aside from the two of them in over three hours.

Melinda and I worked side-by-side the rest of the afternoon, listening to Christmas music while baking cookies, croissants, and donuts, until all orders for Baking Crate had been filled.

"Did you respond to *Festive Treasures*?" Melinda asked as she boxed up the last dozen cookies and began working on the donuts.

"I did. I finally firmed up my decision to enter the cinnamon buns. I am hoping to have Cici fully trained in time for you to help me with the contest. Tomorrow is her first full shift, so we will see how she makes out running the counter."

"I think she will do amazing," Melinda said, putting together two more boxes and filling them while I labeled them all for shipping.

"I hope so because I am going to need to rely on you to make sure the bakery runs while I am prepping for this contest. Not just that, but I am also going to need an assistant for all events of this contest."

"I'm your girl."

The Crispy Biscuit was full by eight the next morning. It had been a good thing that Melinda had come in yesterday, after all, because after the storm, today we were swamped. Between breakfast orders and baking, the three of us hadn't stopped all morning.

Thomas had stopped in early to grab a coffees and muffins for him and Trinity, stating how busy the bookstore was as well. It seemed that the upcoming contest had brought a lot of people into Willow Valley.

"Did you hear? Apparently, the magazine people have arrived," Amanda, one of my regulars, told me as I refilled her coffee.

"That is exciting!" Melinda squealed as she walked by carrying some plates back to the kitchen.

"Yep, they rolled in about an hour ago. They are staying over at the old bed and breakfast on the other side of town," Amanda told us matter-of-factly.

"Oh, that old place?" Melinda questioned. "It's beautiful but it's going to need some updates and soon."

"From what I've heard, it's going to be sold soon," Amanda said.

"Really? Harry and Bessy aren't going to do the renovations on it?" I questioned. They'd owned the Willow Valley Bed and Breakfast since I'd been a little girl.

"Who knows." Amanda shrugged. "Harry's health hasn't been too good, and I think it's a lot on Bessy to run it alone most days."

Just then I noticed a van marked with *Festive Treasures* on the side pull up outside the bakery. A woman got out of the front, followed by a man with a camera. Excitement ran through me as I watched them both pull equipment from the back. I hadn't been expecting them to arrive today, even though I knew they usually did a full-page interview with each of the contestants. I smiled at Amanda and then continued to watch as they made their way to the front door and pulled it open.

"Can I help you?" Melinda asked, going over to them.

"Yes, we are here from *Festive Treasures* to do a piece on Brooke Kinley for the contest."

Melinda clapped her hands with excitement and turned to look at me.

I smiled. "I'm Brooke Kinley."

"Wonderful. Can we take a seat somewhere? We have some questions we'd like to ask you."

Tristan

I HAD BEEN ANNOYED the instant I'd stepped foot into this small town. I was used to staying at the Four Seasons, and this was the farthest away from that. I stood just inside the door to my room at the Willow Valley Bed and Breakfast and looked around. Everything about it was outdated and small. How they expected me to spend eleven days here I had no clue. I placed my suitcase on the bed and then took my laptop over to the small antique desk, setting it up.

"You can't complain about the accommodations," I whispered to myself. I was already under fire by the editor of *Festive Treasures* for cutting up one of their favorite chefs last month in an article. I'd only spoken my mind in what I'd written, stating that I found his meal mediocre at best. How was I supposed to know that he was a personal friend of the editor and that we'd been sent there to do a piece on his new restaurant to help him boost ratings and visibility? Her assistant had approved the article the day she was off but the second she'd gotten the call about the article, I'd been pulled into a meeting. She'd paced back and forth, then screamed at me for a full half hour, then decided to send me here to cover this holiday contest. I am sure this had been my punishment.

I pulled out the file on the contestants and began reading about the first entry. I read over her entry and flipped to the next page, doing the same. I was about four contestants in when I flipped to the next page, only to stop as I read the name on the top of the form. The name was familiar. Could it be? Brooke Kinley from school? I vaguely remembered that she lived in some Valley. I quickly opened my laptop and googled her name, hoping that her picture would appear. The first thing that popped up was The Crispy Biscuit website.

I waited forever for the page to load as I looked to the card that sat beside my computer stating lightning fast internet and chuckled to myself. I may not be able to complain about the accommodations, but I could complain about the internet. How did Vicki expect me to get articles uploaded to the office if the internet was garbage? I let out a sigh when finally, the page loaded, and

I looked over the website. As I read over her site, I noticed a baking crate link and clicked on it, which took me to her catalogue there. She'd gotten herself on Baking Crate? That alone took skill. I'd done articles on some of the best bakers in the world who couldn't get an account there. I scrolled up and looked to the top to her rating where she was recommended as one of the featured bakers there. Impressive, I thought to myself, if it were in fact her.

I went back to her website and found an "about us" page. Clicking the link, slowly her picture appeared. It was her. I sat there staring at her picture. She was still very pretty, and her eyes lit up in her photo. Just then my cell phone pinged and I grabbed it and looked at the message. It was Vicki. She was wondering where I was. They were already over at The Crispy Biscuit, and they were waiting for me to arrive. I swore under my breath, shut my laptop, and grabbed my coat from the back of the chair. The snow had caused the sidewalks to be slippery, and I couldn't find a cab anywhere, so I decided to walk. It took a while, and by the time I'd arrived, they were already finished and were just climbing back into their van.

"Tristan, you're late—again," Vicki said as she dumped her purse into the front seat.

I looked to the editor, my boss, and shrugged. "I'm sorry. I guess time just got away from me."

I could see her clench her jaw. "You know, Tristan, this

is a common occurrence with you. Every. Single. Time," she said, tapping her foot as she looked at me. "I don't think I need to remind you that this is your last chance. You do realize that, don't you? Your last chance to prove to me that you can be good at your job?"

Frank, the camera guy, looked over my way and chuckled to himself, shaking his head while he placed the camera back in the case. I'd worked with Frank on almost everything, and it was no surprise to me that he was laughing and shaking his head.

"Look, I said—" Only she cut me off before I could continue.

"Let me guess, you're sorry, you lost track of time. Well, sorry doesn't cut it any longer. This is it. You blow this one and you're out."

"Yeah, yeah, I get it." I chuckled and rolled my eyes, not believing that she'd actually have the guts to fire me.

"No, to be honest, I don't think you do. I mean it, Tristan, blow it and you'll find out. Now we have a couple of hours, so let's get over to the next contestant's place so we can get their story. As it is, you'll have to go from my notes to write the article on Brooke. I won't have you interrupt her again for another interview."

I looked to Frank after Vicki climbed into the front seat. He shook his head. "You better take her seriously. I don't think I've ever seen her as mad as she was," Frank said, then walked around to the driver's side of the van.

Pissed off, I climbed into the back of the van and shut the door and we took off.

December 1st - The tryouts

I'd been in the small town of Willow Valley for two days, and I still hadn't set foot into The Crispy Biscuit. I'd been working on her article for the magazine from the notes Vicki had taken. Vicki's notes were far more extensive than mine would have been, which made it hard to put my own voice on the article. With every word I wrote, the tension in my neck and my jaw grew tighter. She'd become way more successful than me. She'd followed her dreams, and mine—well, mine had been taken out from underneath me due to my parents' inability to manage their finances correctly.

I'd just deleted the last three paragraphs I'd written when I heard Vicki yell from the hall, "Come on, Tristan, van is leaving in ten minutes!"

I let out a sigh, put my notes down, and grabbed my coat. This morning they were having the tryouts. Since we'd come into such a small town, Vicki thought it would be nice to allow some of the residents to try out as well. A mock contest if you will. So not only were we having the actual contest, but we were holding a smaller version just for fun.

The parking lot to the Willow Valley Town Hall was already packed by the time we'd arrived. I walked in to find the seating on the floor completely full with viewers, talking amongst themselves. I could feel the excitement in the air. I glanced around to see if I could see Brooke, but it was hard with all the people. I followed Vicki up to the stage and took the seat she directed me to.

She walked over to the microphone and gently tapped it, grabbing everyone's attention. "Good morning, people of Willow Valley. We are very excited to get started. If everyone can take their seats, we will start inviting the contestants up on the stage. For the contestants of the actual event that will be held on the twelfth, please note that what they bring today are not their actual entry items for the contest. This is a simple run-through to make sure everything goes well."

While everyone took their seat, Vicki walked over to me. "You better have brought your notebook. I want a short article written about each of the smaller contestants as well. We do, after all, have prizes for them."

I reached into my coat pocket, my eyes never leaving Vicki's, and pulled out my small notebook, flipping it open. "Happy?"

She gave me the look she always did and then turned and walked back over to the microphone. "Okay, our first contestants are three entries from the local town of Willow Valley. Bessy Tulip, owner of the Willow Valley Bed and Breakfast, she has entered her Mint Chip Cookies. Diana Granger has entered her Butternut Jingle Balls, and Mindi Potts has entered her Santa's Kisses. Ladies, come on up with your entries and place them on the table for our judges."

I watched as all three ladies approached the stage and climbed the stairs. Diana and Mindi were up first, and Bessy followed behind. Vicki walked over to the table and took a bite of the first cookie, then moved on to the next and the last, taking her time to taste each one. In a matter of minutes, she announced the winners, and I feverishly marked them down in the order announced. Third place went to Bessy, second to Diana, and the winner of the resident portion of Willow Valley was Mindi. Vicki gave each contestant the appropriate ribbon, followed by a large gift basket, as the crowd cheered.

"Well, that was exciting," she said into the microphone as she returned to her spot, while clapping as the ladies left the stage.

"Now on to the tryouts for the contestants of the *Festive Treasures* contest." Vicki turned to look in my direction just as I let out a yawn.

I quickly composed myself as her eyes met mine. I could tell from the look that she was pissed.

"All right, first we have Andrea Linden from The

Buttery Croissant from New York. Andrea has worked in some of the finest bakeries and restaurants all over the world. She started her venture in 2010. She opened The Buttery Croissant in 2015 and has won numerous awards in the past few years, including 2020's and 2021's *Festive Treasures Award*. She has brought her Linzer Cookies for today. Andrea, please come up on the stage."

I glanced to the steps, watching as Andrea climbed them carrying her plate of cookies. Then I glanced to the girls who were still in line. I didn't see Brooke anywhere. I frowned. Had she decided not to bother showing up?

"Next we have Jennifer Weber from The Happening Place in Florida. Jennifer is a self-taught baker. She started The Happening Place in 2019. In 2021 she won the Local Best Bakery Award. This is her first time entering into the *Festive Treasures* contest. She has brought her soft and chewy ginger cookies for today. Jennifer..."

Again, I glanced in the direction of the stairs. There was only one contestant standing there now. Had Brooke backed out, I wondered.

"Polly Campbell from Campbell's Bakery in Denver. Polly originally hales from Paris where she studied in one of the bakery world's finest schools. She opened Campbell's Bakery in 2014 and has won local awards each year. This is her first time entering *Festive Treasures*' contest. She has brought with her Pecan Shortbread Cookies. Polly..."

As Polly climbed the stairs, I noticed no one else stood in line. I couldn't help but smirk. I didn't think she'd have the guts to appear, and I chuckled to myself.

Vicki cleared her throat. "Last we have Willow Valley's own Brooke Kinley, owner of The Crispy Biscuit."

The crowd cheered and clapped, and I looked over to the stairs, but still she hadn't appeared.

"Brooke took over The Crispy Biscuit in 2018 after her parents retired. Originally a small breakfast diner, after she'd completed her culinary and pastry diploma, she added a bakery portion to the small diner. Not only is she a success with *Festive Treasures*, winning the third place in 2020's and second place winner in 2021's *Festive Treasure* event, but she is also the only contestant that has a Baking Crate account. She has decided to enter her Grinch-A-Mas Cookies for today."

I placed my hands behind my head, a smirk on my face, certain that Brooke was not going to show up as the crowd cheered and clapped. I'd just closed my eyes and stuck both feet out to cross them as I reclined in the chair when I felt someone hit my feet, followed by a loud scream. Horrified, I opened my eyes to see cookies all over the floor of the stage, and a woman in a pile on the floor.

Vicki looked horrified, and Frank looked shocked. All I could do was sit there staring at the scene before me. Before I knew what was happening, people from everywhere came running over to Brooke, while I sat on the chair I'd been told to sit in.

"Tristan, I don't want to hear it," Vicki said as she wrapped her coat tighter around her as we watched the ambulance pull away.

I'd been trying to explain to Vicki how it had been an accident, but she didn't want to hear it. She'd whispered something to Frank, who took her arm and began leading her back inside, when I stopped her.

"Seriously, it wasn't like I stuck my foot out on purpose."

"Tristan, we have it on tape. You better hope the hell you didn't do it on purpose. However, I can assure you that I will be reviewing it to see what the hell happened. It may be our only chance to get out of a lawsuit."

"Oh come on, Vicki. No one is going to sue anyone," I said with annoyance.

"Really? The woman was knocked unconscious, not to mention any other injuries she may have gotten. What do you think is going to happen," Vicki demanded.

"The woman tripped...and you're blaming me, worried that you're going to get sued!" I shouted.

"She tripped over your feet! I warned you, Tristan, one more fuck-up and you were done. I swear you'd better hope I don't find any evidence of you tripping that woman on the video or you are finished. Also, you'd best hope there isn't a lawsuit. Now I have work to go and do. You just get out of my sight for a while."

Once Vicki left, I stood in the middle of the parking lot alone, aside from a few residents of Willow Valley, who stood in small circles, no doubt talking about what had happened. I debated going back inside, but Vicki's words stuck at the forefront of my mind. She didn't want to see me, and since she was worried about being sued, I decided that perhaps I should head to the hospital and make sure that Brooke was, in fact, okay. That way I could try and figure out what her injuries were and if she was indeed thinking of suing. Maybe I could even talk her out of going after the magazine or me. I made my way over to two women who stood whispering to one another as they looked my way.

"Excuse me, ladies. You wouldn't happen to know the number for a cab company would you?"

"There are no local cab companies in Willow Valley," one of them answered.

"Oh, my boss wanted me to head over to the hospital and make sure Brooke is okay. You know, after the fall," I lied.

They looked to one another. "We can take you," one said.

The other said, "I'm Peggy Hollis, and this is Trinity Foster."

I nodded to both women and followed them to their vehicle.

Brooke

MY HEAD WAS THROBBING, and I could hear murmured conversations in the room. I slowly opened my eyes, the bright lights hurting. As the voices continued, I wished that whoever was speaking would stop. As the room came into view, nothing about it seemed familiar and I frowned, first looking down to the bottom of the bed where I saw my right foot in an air cast.

"Oh my goodness, she's awake!" I heard a familiar voice exclaim.

I looked to the left and saw Melinda coming over to my side.

"We were so worried about you," she said, taking hold of my hand.

"What happened?" I questioned, looking back down to my foot.

"Oh, Brooke, it was horrible. You had an accident at the bake-off tryouts. You tripped, fell, hit your head, and well, you have a severely sprained ankle," she cried.

It was all slowly coming back to me. I'd been running late and had been rushing into the auditorium. I walked in just as they were just announcing me. I'd ripped the clear wrap off the plate of cookies I'd been carrying, bolted up the side of the auditorium to the staircase at the bottom of the stage, and rushed up the stairs. I'd just gotten to the top and was on my way across the stage when I tripped over something. Cookies went flying and so did I.

"God, I remember it now. I've made a complete ass of myself." I cried, burying my face into my hands. "Did everyone see it happen? Does anyone know what it was I tripped on?" I questioned.

Melinda looked to me and then over to the other side of the room without saying anything. Her eyes reverted back to mine. I knew she knew what had happened.

"What? What is it, Melinda?"

"He tripped you!" she exclaimed, looking over to the other side of the room again.

"Who?" I questioned. I hadn't seen anyone in the room with us.

"I did not! How dare you accuse me," a deep voice cried out. "It was an accident. I'd never do such a thing on purpose."

I glanced to my right to see Tristan Ryan step into my

view. What the hell was he doing here? I clenched my jaw and looked back to Melinda, about to say something, when the door to my room opened and in walked a man in a white lab coat.

"Brooke, good to see you're awake," he said, coming over and sitting down on the edge of my bed. "Could I have a little space here please."

Both Melinda and Tristan took a step back, and I looked to the man who must have been the one taking care of me.

"So, Brooke, any headache?"

I shook my head. "No. Well, perhaps a small one, but nothing I'd be concerned with," I said.

"Well, you hit your head when you fell, so I just wanted to be sure. There is a slight bruise on your forehead, no bump, but nothing that shouldn't heal up in a few days."

"What about my foot? I have a diner and bakery to run," I said, looking down at the horrible walking boot. "It's the holidays. I have to work. There is no way I can be down for the count during this time of year," I cried, panicking.

"Well that, my dear, is going to be on a little longer than a couple of days."

"How long?" I cried.

"Well, it's a very severe sprain. You'll need to be off your foot for at least a week, perhaps two. Then after that, you'll be on crutches. I'd say overall, it will probably be five to six weeks before you can walk without crutches, and then probably another four to five before it will feel completely normal," he said, closing the file he held in his hand.

"I cannot be off my feet for a day let alone a week."

"I'm sorry, Brooke, but it's a bad injury."

"No. You don't understand. I have a diner and bakery to run. I have accounts, I have a contest, I have—"

"Brooke, I can help you," Melinda said, trying to calm me.

"Thank you, Melinda, I appreciate it, but I can't put all this onto you. This is my responsibility. It's my business, my livelihood. I have to work."

Melinda looked at me, her eyes full of concern.

"Brooke, if you don't follow my orders, you'll be off much longer than what I've already figured. As it is, it's not written in stone. Now, give me some time and we will get all the paperwork in order to send you home," the doctor said just before walking out of the room.

Panic hit me all at once and I found it hard to breathe. I could already imagine the pile of orders that had come in from Baking Crate, not to mention how many orders our residents had dropped off for their Christmas events.

"This can't be happening. Nonononono..." I cried as I buried my face in my hands.

"Brooke, seriously, I've got it under control," Melinda

said, rubbing my back. "I will make sure everything is taken care of. This is what you trained me for. It will be fine."

Everything was running through my mind at a million miles per minute. Then it all came crashing down as Tristan Ryan stepped into my view. I glared at him as he stood there in his over-priced sweater and perfectly tailored suit pants, not saying a word.

"You...of all people."

Tristan looked over his shoulder as if I were talking to someone behind him. When he was satisfied no one was there, he looked at me. "What?"

"What? What do you mean what? Just look at what you've done!" I cried.

"What I've done? Oh no, I haven't done anything. You are the one who tripped!"

I shook my head, not believing what I was hearing. I glared at him. "I see you haven't changed much at all! You trip me, and now it's me who has done this! Like I wanted to trip. Makes me remember back to the days in school when you were always messing up but never taking the blame."

"You guys. Please...there is no need to fight," Melinda cried.

"Oh no, you're wrong, there is a need to fight. With him, there is always a need," I bit out.

A shrill ring rang through the room, and Tristan

pulled his phone from his pocket and looked down to the screen. "I've got to take this," he mumbled.

"So take it," I barked.

The tension within me finally lowered as he left the room. I leaned back against the pillow behind me and looked to Melinda, not knowing what to do. There was no way I could put all of this on her. "Don't worry, I'll figure something out," I whispered.

I sat on the edge of the hospital bed going over my order schedule. While I'd been waiting for discharge, I decided that I would try to figure out how I was going to get everything completed. I'd had twenty orders come in on Baking Crate today alone, and I'd just gotten off the phone with Cici, who'd told me that there had been five orders placed for holiday parties.

"Well? Come up with anything?" Melinda asked, coming back into the room with two bottles of orange juice.

"It's impossible. There is no way you can handle all this on your own," I cried, looking down at the piece of paper I'd been using to try and make sense of everything.

"No matter how many times I try to cut it, orders will have to be canceled."

"What about your mom? Maybe she can come and help me?"

"No, her and Dad have gone off to Paris. They left two days ago, and they won't be back until well into January. Which, by then, I'll have messed up enough to lose my Baking Crate account."

Melinda looked at me with sympathy. "I can try, Brooke."

"This is just a disaster," I said, throwing the pencil down on the bed.

Melinda grabbed the paper and pencil and looked at it. "Let me see if I can't figure something out," she said, putting the end of the pencil in her mouth.

"Well, are you ready to head out?" the doctor asked, stepping back into the room.

I nodded, swallowing hard at the thought of what I was about to lose.

"I'm just going to go down and pull the car around," Melinda said, nodding to the doctor.

"I'll get a wheelchair. You can just come take her once you're back. Here is a prescription for pain, and your crutches are on the way up." He smiled. "And a mild prescription to help with the anxiety you are feeling."

I tore the prescriptions from his hand and shoved them into my purse, mumbling under my breath. It wasn't long before I sat in a wheelchair as Melinda pushed me through the halls of the hospital. My head ached, and I hoped it would pass once I'd gotten home and could think through things a little more logically. We were just about to the front doors of the hospital when Tristan appeared.

"Going home?" he asked.

"Oh, not you again," I gritted. "Could you please just go away."

"He can't. I told him we would give him a ride back into town," Melinda said from behind me.

"What? Why?"

"Well he was nice enough to come out here to check up on you. It was the least I could do." Melinda stopped to help me get into my winter coat.

"Melinda, knowing Tristan, he probably came out here because he is in trouble and was told to smooth things over," I gritted.

"Brooke, be nice. He was trying to be nice," Melinda whispered to me as she began pushing me to the car.

"If you knew him like I know him, there isn't a nice bone in his body. He only does things to protect one person, himself."

I looked out the window as we drove through Willow Valley. Christmas lights sparkled against the falling snow, and all storefronts looked almost magical. Even though I was feeling down about everything, this ride had lifted my spirits a little. I watched as Melinda drove. She was headed toward my home, and I frowned.

"Are you dropping him off first?" I questioned?

Melinda shook her head. "No, I figured you'd want to get home and get settled first. So..."

The last thing I wanted was for Tristan Ryan to set foot into my home. "No, I'm okay, we can take Tristan back to the inn first."

"Nonsense, we will get you settled first," he said from the back seat.

My jaw clenched at the sound of his voice. He'd been really quiet during the entire ride back into Willow Valley, and I'd really hoped he'd continue to be.

I was about to protest again when Melinda pulled the car into my small driveway and came to a stop right in front of my little house that was tucked in behind The Crispy Biscuit.

I let out a sigh as both of them got out of the car first and watched as they walked around the front to my side. Tristan opened the door and held his hand out for me to take. I didn't want help from him so I shoved his hand out of the way. "I can do it," I barked.

"Suit yourself." He took a step back, giving me room to climb out of the car.

I placed both hands on the sides of the car and tried to pull myself out. I tried to push off with my good foot, only to realize that I'd be putting pressure on my sprained one, then I tried to switch and stopped immediately.

"Having trouble?" he asked, leaning down and looking into the car at me.

"No." I frowned. Was he making fun of me? I sucked in a breath as he stood there looking at me. I didn't want to do it, but I knew I had to ask for his help. "Just give me your hand."

"What? Is Brooke Kinley actually asking for my help?" he asked, holding his hand to his chest.

I glared at him as a gust of wind blew more snow around. "Seriously, just give me your hand."

He held his large hand out for me to take, and as I slid forward, he wrapped his other arm securely around my waist, practically lifting me out of the car. Immediately, I placed one hand on the car door and the other on the car, expecting him to let me go, only he didn't.

"You can let me go now," I grumbled.

"I can? Exactly how do you expect to get from here to the house?"

I looked at the ground. It was covered in deep snow, and no doubt underneath was a layer of ice. "Crutches," I blurted.

"I don't think you should, Brooke. It's slippery," Melinda said, sliding as she returned from unlocking the front door. "What if you fall?"

"I won't. Now, the crutches please." I looked to

Melinda, waiting for her to get them from the trunk of the car. She glanced to Tristan and then back to me and then went to the trunk and pulled them out, handing them to me.

I had barely taken two steps when one of the crutches slipped out from underneath me. I let out a scream, and Tristan grabbed me just before I went down. I leaned back against his chest, trying hard to compose myself and stop shaking.

"Okay, are you finished being stubborn now?" he asked, his breath tickling my ear.

I clenched my jaw and nodded my head. The cocky smile I remembered appeared as he slowly let me go. He wrapped one arm around my waist and carefully guided me to the door.

Tristan

I STEPPED INSIDE and looked around at Brooke's small home. Everything was neatly organized and mostly decorated for Christmas. It had one thing that my place did not, nor any home I'd grown up in: a feeling of home, of warmth. Even though it appeared that everything had its place, it still felt lived in, whereas mine had always felt like a museum. I thought back to my two-bedroom New York apartment and realized it still felt that way.

"You can just put my coat on the back of the dining room chair," Brooke said as she shrugged out of her winter coat. Melinda struggled to grab her coat and hold onto Brooke at the same time, so I quickly reached and took the coat.

"Did you want to get changed?" Melinda questioned.

"Yes, and I'd really love a cup of tea," Brooke said.

Melinda turned toward me. "Do you think you could make her a cup of tea while I help her get changed?"

I looked around. Was she speaking to me?

"Don't ask him to do anything. I'd rather crawl to the kitchen and make it after you leave," Brooke said, eying me.

"I can make you a cup of tea, Brooke," I grunted. "I'm not totally useless." I slipped out of my jacket, placing it on the coat rack by the door.

"No, I'll give you that. You're not totally useless. If you were, I'd be walking just fine."

"I didn't trip you, and if you insist I did it wasn't done on purpose, Brooke," I grunted.

Brooke shook her head and whispered something to Melinda. They both looked at me, and then Melinda wrapped her arm around Brooke's waist and helped her to the bedroom. Just as they got to the door, Melinda turned and looked back at me, signaling that I should get into the kitchen.

I looked around, finally seeing the kettle on the counter, and made my way over, checking to see if it was full of water, which it was, so I turned it on and leaned against the counter.

While I waited, I pulled my phone from my pocket and checked my email. The only one that appeared was from Vicki. I was hesitant to read it, but knew if it was something I had to respond to, I'd best get it done. She had sent it to me sometime between me arriving at the hospital and now, demanding that I did whatever it took to avoid a lawsuit, or I was out of a job. I blew out a breath. To be honest, I felt somewhat panicked that after all these years I could be back to applying for jobs.

I quickly logged into my online banking, I needed to see where I stood. If I did get fired, I wanted to make sure I knew how much I had to last me. Immediately, my heart sank. Staring back at me, my account was overdrawn, and my credit card had more on it than was safe or sane. It was simple, I was broke. There was no way I could afford to lose my job. There was also no way I could afford to spend one more night at that inn either, since the magazine wouldn't allow me to submit an expense report until the end of the month.

I flipped to my email and hit reply to Vicki, letting her know I was doing my best to make things right. Then I pocketed my phone and let out a sigh just as the kettle boiled. I quickly switched it off and opened the cupboard door above the kettle. There staring me in the face were Crispy Biscuit branded mugs. I took the first one I saw and turned it around to see 'Warm wishes and Marshmallow kisses' written on the opposite side.

Cute, I thought to myself, then I dug around until I found a box of chamomile tea and plopped the bag in the cup pouring the water over it. Then I took the cup and carried it into the living room.

Brooke had just sat down on the couch, her foot propped up. I placed the mug down on the table.

"Melinda, can you bring me my purse, and that notebook I was working out of please," Brooke asked, pointing over toward the door where her purse sat.

Melinda scurried over and grabbed both, placing them down on the couch beside her. "What are you doing?" she questioned.

"What I was doing before: seeing if there is anything I can cancel or push back."

"I told you I'd handle it," Melinda gritted.

"I appreciate the offer. However, the pair of us barely made it through last Christmas. Cici doesn't know anything about baking, and well, the other kitchen staff are for the diner. It's you and me only. One week from today is the contest. That I can drop out of, but it's all these orders I'm concerned with," Brooke said, holding up what appeared to me to be a very small list.

"That's it?" I questioned. "That list is what you are worried about?"

She slowly turned her head in my direction and glared at me. Then she shook her head. "This is only the beginning. I haven't checked at what has still come in since three this afternoon. It could easily be tripled."

"I'll go get started on these right now," Melinda said, taking the list from Brooke and reading it.

"No, it's been a long day, Melinda. I'll need you

tomorrow. Besides, you still need to take Tristan back to the inn before you get home and get some rest. It's getting late. I'll give it a try in the kitchen tomorrow. If I must sit on a chair, so be it. Otherwise, I see no other option but to close down the pastry side of The Crispy Biscuit until I can walk or I'll just close the Baking Crate store."

I could see the worry all over Brooke's face as we all stood there in silence.

"It took me so much hard work to even get an account with them," she muttered. "Hours upon hours of hard work. Dedication, proof that I wouldn't fuck it up."

Melinda knelt to try and comfort her. I stood there, not knowing what to say, just watching as a tear slid down her cheek. I felt I had to do something, but what? And then the words from Vicki's email ran through my mind. *Do whatever it takes not to get the magazine sued.*

"You don't need to close anything," I announced.

Both Melinda and Brooke looked at me, frowning. "What would you know about it," Brooke bit out between sniffles.

"Well, I have an idea."

"Great, I can't wait to hear this." Brooke flopped back against the pillows and rolled her eyes.

I blew out a breath. "How about I stay here. I can take care of things around here, and help with the bakery. It's the least I can do after what happened."

Melinda gave me a soft smile, but Brooke just scowled.

"I don't think that is the answer at all. You, Tristan, need to go back to the inn and stay as far away as possible from me and my business."

I shook my head. "Look, I have the skill needed to bake for the bakery, and honestly, you are going to need help here. You can't walk at all, and you even said it yourself, your new employee, Cicil, can't bake."

Brooke looked at me as if I were crazy and shook her head. "Her name is Cici! And no, Tristan, I live in a one-bedroom house. There isn't room."

"It's fine. I'll sleep right here, on the couch. You won't even know I'm here. I'll be up early and be at the bakery," I stated.

"You know nothing about what is needed at the bakery. You work for a magazine."

"Melinda, can help me. Right?" I said, turning and looking in her direction.

She looked back at me. Even she looked shocked that I was offering this.

Brooke looked to Melinda and shook her head. Then she turned her attention back to her notebook and began writing some things down.

"Seriously, Brooke, I can do this."

"I seriously doubt it," she said through clenched teeth.

"I'm asking you to trust me on this."

"Trust you. Ha, that is funny. Trust you, the man who ruined every single solitary recipe we had to make together in school, the man who chastised me for wanting to follow my dreams, and the man who tripped me, purposely or accidently, whichever it was, simply to ruin my chances of winning a contest. I'm supposed to trust you!" Brooke said, turning her head away from me.

"Brooke, don't be so..."

"Don't be so...what, Melinda? Remember, I know him!"

"Brooke, you said yourself, I can't do this on my own. If he can bake, then perhaps he can be of some help. You never know."

I could see the irritation growing on Brooke's face. Finally, she threw her hands up in the air. "Fine, fine. Tristan, welcome to the couch."

"I'm glad to see you've accepted that I'm right. Melinda, can you take me over to the inn to grab my things?"

Melinda nodded and was just about to put her coat on when Brooke chuckled.

"See, Melinda, that right there. I'm glad to see you've accepted that I'm right," she mocked. "That is the exact reason why I don't want his help."

Melinda leaned down and whispered something into Brooke's ear and then nodded to the doorway. "We'll be right back."

Within an hour, I'd checked out of the inn, and we'd returned to Brooke's. The three of us now sat in Brooke's living room as she went over all the orders that had come in. She seemed a little bit calmer than she was when I left, which was a good thing. I sipped on a cup of coffee while they began planning how to attack everything in the morning. As soon as they were finished, Melinda got up and put her coat on.

"I'll see you tomorrow. I'll be here around four," she said, glancing to her watch.

"Five!" Brooke yelled.

"Five," Melinda corrected.

I walked her to the door, locking it behind her, and turned back to see Brooke struggling to get up.

"Here, let me help you," I said, rushing over to her side.

She shook her head and held out her hand, but I didn't give up. Instead, I held out my hand and waited for her to take it. "Help me to the bedroom."

I placed my arm securely around her waist and slowly we made our way into her bedroom. I pulled the blankets back for her and helped her to get seated on the bed.

"Need anything else?" I asked.

"I'll get what I need from the dresser," she grumbled.

I looked to the other side of the room where her dresser stood against the far wall. "What do you need?" I said again, this time my voice more demanding.

She let out a huff. "Top drawer, flannel pajamas, and don't you dare look at anything else."

I walked over and pulled the top drawer open. There on top was a pair of white flannel pajamas covered in little puppies wearing a Santa hat. I couldn't help but smile as I reached in and grabbed the pair on top. "You actually wear these?" I questioned, holding them up.

"Tristan," she gritted, her jaw clenched.

Immediately, I wiped the smile from my face and placed them down at the foot of the bed. "Need anything else?" I questioned.

"Glass of water."

"Okay." I turned and left the room, grabbing a glass of water from the kitchen, and made my way back and set it on her night table. Then I switched the small light on beside her bed and shut the overhead light off. "Anything else?"

She looked around the bedroom. "My book. It's out on the table beside the couch."

I darted out and picked up the book from the small table and carried it back into her while looking at the cover.

"You actually read that filth?" I said, holding up the book to produce a romance cover.

"Yes, and I happen to like it. There are sheets and extra blankets in the closet beside the bathroom."

I nodded and turned to leave her bedroom, pulling the door shut, but I stopped and turned back to her. "Brooke,

I'm glad you've come to your senses and saw that I was right."

"Oh…is that what you think has happened here?"

I nodded.

"Don't flatter yourself. I am exhausted, in pain, and was tired of arguing." I met her eyes as she glared at me. "Close my door."

I pulled the door closed and stood there for a moment, and as I looked around the small living room, I realized that I'd always been a fuckup. My brother had firmly reminded me of that ever since the day he'd found out what I'd done with my tuition, taking what was earmarked for school, paying for only the first semester, and pocketing the rest so I could party it up. However, the second I'd laid eyes on Brooke again, I wanted to change that about myself. I hoped that I could prove to her that I wasn't the fuckup everyone knew I was, but, deep down, I knew she already thought that of me. My heart sank. I'd just have to prove to her she was wrong, and it all started with tomorrow.

Brooke

I'D BEEN in bed only a half hour. I'd tried to read but couldn't get my mind off tomorrow. Panic had set in. They only had three hours before the diner opened at eight, when Melinda would be pulled from the kitchen to help Cici with tables. The orders had piled up. When I last checked my Baking Crate orders, there was way more than I would even be comfortable with. I felt bad knowing that not only would she have to deal with all that, but that she also had to deal with Tristan and getting him to learn the ins and outs of what I'd taught her over the past few years.

I let out a sigh and stared up at the ceiling. I needed a Christmas miracle at this point because I feared the worst. I rolled onto my side. Light from the living room spilled under the door. Tristan was still up. I clenched my teeth, worried that he wouldn't be up in time to meet Melinda at five. I felt so helpless.

I rolled onto my back. I had to use the bathroom. I looked to the bathroom door. It wasn't that far. Surely, I could make it a couple of steps on my own, I thought to myself. I kicked the covers off and sat up, placing my good foot down on the carpeted floor. I stood up and steadied myself, then placed my sprained foot down. Instantly, pain shot up my leg, and I let out a yelp.

"Brooke? You okay?" Tristan's deep voice yelled from the other side of the door.

I bit my bottom lip to try and stop the tears from forming in my eyes and choked out a yes. I was about to sit back down when the bedroom door opened. I looked over my shoulder to see Tristan looking in at me.

"What are you doing?" he questioned.

"I needed to use the washroom," I whimpered, holding onto my leg just above the air cast.

"So, why didn't you call for me."

"I'm not going to call you in the middle of the night and wake you up. That's ridiculous."

"It's only eleven. I'm still up," he said, stepping inside my room. I felt his hands go around my waist, and he pulled me back against him. "Stop being so stubborn," he whispered, his breath tickling my ear, as he guided me to the bathroom.

I wanted to die as he left me in the washroom to do

my business. "Just call me when you are finished," he said, pulling the door closed behind him.

Once I'd called, he helped me back to the bed and I crawled in. I grabbed my prescription and popped one of the pain pills into my mouth and took a drink of water, while Tristan placed the covers on me, making sure there wasn't a ton of pressure on my foot.

"Do you need anything else?" he asked.

"I want to talk to you," I murmured, looking at him.

"About?"

"I'm worried about tomorrow."

"Why?"

I adjusted my pillows behind my back and leaned against them. "Well, it's just there is so much to do, and you don't know any of it."

"I can learn, Brooke."

"I know. I guess I'd just feel better if you'd let me bring you up-to-date on what's involved." I shrugged.

"Okay."

"Well first, Baking Crate orders, they are super important. They have to be done and ready to be shipped, and that is where the extra care comes in. They have to be put in a box and wrapped with The Crispy Biscuit paper, then placed securely into the Baking Crate boxes, and packed perfectly, so they are protected. They need to be labeled, and then Fred from the delivery company picks them up somewhere around ten. But they need to be done way before ten because once all that stuff is baked, you need to make sure that the counters are full for open, which is at eight. The kitchen staff for the diner, they know what to do. Greg has been here since my parents owned the place. He's the chef, so you don't need to worry about that side of things. He can take care of all that."

"Okay, so bake, pack, get ready for shipment, and make sure the bakery cases are full for open. Got it." He smiled.

"Well, I make it sound easy, but really there is much more to it than that."

"Melinda is going to be there, right?"

"Yes." I nodded.

"Okay, so I'll watch her. It will be fine."

"She'll be here, except on her days off. That is where you'll need to know how to do everything on your own. You'll need to know how to bake everything, and you'll need to have excellent time management skills."

"It will be fine," he said, trying to assure me again, but I was still feeling uneasy.

"Look, I have an instruction booklet," I said, reaching over to my nightstand and opening the drawer, pulling out a pink book.

"Looks like you've thought of everything." He chuckled.

"That's because it's important." I nodded, opening the book and flipping through the pages and pages of handwritten notes I'd made. "I had to come up with this, in case of an emergency. You know, a worst-case scenario sort of thing, and well, you're here now...so..."

"Are you saying I'm a worst-case scenario?" Tristan asked, trying to meet my eyes.

I fought back tears as I met his eyes and nodded. I was not used to giving up control of something I'd worked so hard to build. I ran my hand over the cover of the pink notebook and let out a yawn.

"You're exhausted, and I'd better get to sleep," Tristan said, slipping the notebook from my hands. "My alarm goes off at four," he mumbled as he got up off the edge of the bed and walked over to the door.

"Please, Tristan, don't let me down."

He said nothing. Instead, he pulled the door closed behind him, and shortly thereafter, the lights on the other side of the door went out. I slid down under the covers, then pulled them up around my neck and closed my eyes. I said a silent prayer that everything would work out for the best, but still somewhere deep inside of me, I was worried that this Christmas would be a total disaster.

Tristan

As I FLIPPED through the pages of Brooke's notebook, I realized just how far out of my element I was. It hadn't mattered how many years had passed, she had always made me feel nervous, and now it was even worse. She had become highly successful. I'd checked her out on social media a few times over the last few days, and I'd checked out her Instagram account today and had gotten lost in watching some of her videos.

I was so impressed by her, by the care she took with everything she did. In every single video, she was smiling and happy, laughing. She even baked with a smile on her face, just like she had done in school. She truly had a love for what she did. I had just wanted notoriety.

I reached up and shut the light off at the end of the couch and placed the notebook down on the table. I put my arm behind my head and stared up at the ceiling. I knew that come tomorrow I would be insufferable. I wasn't used to getting up before dawn. I was used to my life at the magazine, strolling into the office around eleven, latte or coffee in hand, and doing the bare minimum required of me every single day to continue providing myself a paycheck.

Although, as soon as I closed my eyes, I saw Brooke's—worry lining her face as she sat on the couch tonight, and again only a few short minutes ago while I sat there assuring her everything would be fine when, in fact, I had no idea if it would be or not. I hadn't picked up a spatula or turned a mixer on since school, which I hadn't even finished. I had no idea what it was I'd gotten myself into, and judging from her notebook, it was way more than I'd bargained for. Then the worry crept in. I was going to let her down, just like I'd let everyone down in my entire family, and I hadn't even started yet. I was going to make an already bad situation worse.

It felt as if I'd barely closed my eyes when the shrill ring of the alarm clock went off. I reached over and shut the noise off that rang through the room. I flung my arm over my eyes and prayed for death; it was way too early to get up. I felt sick to my stomach as I kicked the covers off myself, the cool air greeting me. I sat up and wiped my hand over my face, then I heard a noise from the bedroom. I listened again; sure I heard her moving around.

"Brooke?" I called.

"I need to use the bathroom again!" she yelled back.

I glanced around the dark room, forgetting where I'd put my jeans, and looked down at myself, shirtless and in boxers. Well, if I was going to be staying here and helping her get around, I wasn't going to be getting dressed in the middle of the night every time she needed something, I thought to myself and got up.

I opened the door and saw she had once again tried to get out of bed on her own. I chuckled to myself and walked over, wrapping my arm once again around her waist, helping her to the washroom. Once she was finished and I opened the door, I noticed her eyes fall to my chest then to my abs, and I saw a slight blush fall across her cheeks.

"Like what you see, perhaps?" I questioned.

"Don't flatter yourself. Next time get dressed," she grumbled.

"Come on, cranky. Let's get you back to bed."

"I'm not going back to bed. It's time to get up."

I helped her back to the bed and got her clothes out and left her to get dressed, while I myself got dressed. Then we sat together at the kitchen table. I'd made her coffee and toast and stood looking out the back window as I drank down my coffee.

"Well, I just saw Melinda open the back door. I guess

I'll get you settled on the couch with everything you need and head on over."

I opened the back door to the bakery and stepped inside, happy to feel the warmth hit me. The bright lights of the kitchen hurt my eyes and it took a minute to allow them to adjust. Melinda stood behind one of the counters, already mixing something in a bowl, while a large floor mixer ran. She'd only been in here for fifteen minutes and she'd already accomplished so much, I thought. I looked around. It had been many years since I'd stepped foot in a kitchen, and from what I could remember, I wasn't very good at it.

"Good morning!" Melinda sang as she continued to mix some ingredients together in the bowl in front of her.

"Morning."

"So, I already got things started. I figured the easiest way to go about this would be for me to do the baking and you can do the packaging."

"No need. Brooke gave me her guide. I went over things. I can at least help with the chocolate chip cookies. They were pretty straight forward."

Melinda smiled. "Okay, well, we need a bunch of

those, so I guess you can start the other mixer. Did she give you her recipe?"

I nodded, pulling the book out from my back pocket and flipping to the page that contained the recipe.

"Okay, well, all ingredients are on the shelf over there. Let me know if you run out of something, or if it gets low, so I can put it on our order sheet."

"Got it!" I said, pulling down a bag of flour.

As I began dumping things into the mixer, I noticed Melinda watching my every move. I did my best to ignore it, but when I could feel her stare burning into me, I turned and looked at her. "What?"

"Um...nothing," she said, turning back to her bowl.

"No, what is it?"

"Well, it's just you're supposed to start by beating the butter, sugar, and eggs together, then you add in dry ingredients."

"Well, I've always done it this way, and it's always come together for me," I said, continuing to dump copious amounts of ingredients into the bowl of the large floor mixer.

"Okay. As I said, it's nothing," Melinda said, turning back to her bowl, beginning to work a little faster.

As I'd gotten all the ingredients in, I took the bag of flour and began pouring. Soon I was surrounded by a cloud of white dust, and as the air cleared, I once again saw Melinda watching me as she piped cookie after cookie on the sheet in front of her. I smiled at her and flipped the switch on the mixer, which only made that cloud of flour worse and made the white powdery stuff fly out of the bowl, coating almost everything around it.

I coughed then smiled as I watched as the ingredients somewhat came together. When I stopped the mixer, I noticed large chunks of butter that hadn't mixed in well. Then I grabbed the bag of chocolate chips and began to pour, turning the mixer on again.

Once I had the cookie dough ready, I wheeled the large bowl over to the counter and grabbed one of the large baking sheets Melinda had prepared and began spooning out the dough and dropping them onto the pan. Melinda had already pulled croissants, macarons, and the cocoa cuddles from the oven, along with some cinnamon donuts.

She looked down at the tray, a look of horror on her face. "Tristan, these all need to be uniform size. They can't go like that." She grabbed one of the dough balls and ripped it apart in her hand, a funny look lining her face as she took a closer look at the dough.

"What?"

"Tristan, the butter isn't even mixed in. It's literally in chunks," she said, looking into the bowl. "And this dough is way too sticky. It has nowhere near enough flour," she said, trying to shake the dough from her hand.

"Oh well, not a problem. I can add more," I said.

"Well how much did you already put in?" she asked, scooping more of the dough out and looking more closely at it.

"Oh, I don't know, about half a bag." I shrugged.

"The recipe for this size calls for..." She mentally calculated it. "Oh man...I don't even know off the top of my head. I'd have to calculate it...but it's supposed to make 1440 cookies...or 120 dozen," she said with frustration.

"Okay, so I'll add more." I shrugged, heading for the flour.

"No...please...I'll take charge of these. This dough is garbage. Why don't you package up these orders to go to Baking Crate. Leave the boxes unsealed so I can make sure they are done correctly."

I watched her as she wheeled the large mixing bowl across the kitchen and dumped all the dough into the garbage, and then she washed the bowl and began again. While I packaged up each of the orders, I watched her as she measured out each of the ingredients, mixing them in at the appropriate times.

As the morning went on, other staff began arriving, and then soon we were open. Melinda continued baking at a furious pace, while I continued boxing up the Baking Crate orders. When I was finished, I took out trays of cookies and popped them into the display cases and made my way back into the kitchen where Melinda was checking over my packing skills.

"Well?" I questioned.

"These look pretty good," she said, going over the boxes I'd done. "Now they have to go into these Baking Crate boxes, and once in there, you're going to pack this shredded paper around the box, making sure that it's snug inside and cannot move," she said, shoving handfuls of paper around the Crispy Biscuit branded boxes.

Who didn't know how to stuff a box, I thought to myself. So, once she went back to what she had been working on, I began stuffing the boxes with paper and taping them shut with the special labels that I'd been told to use.

We'd continued working until three in the afternoon when, completely exhausted, I slid into a chair with a cup of coffee. All of the other kitchen staff that ran the diner were gone, their areas already cleaned.

"What on earth are you doing?" Melinda questioned, coming back in from serving a customer.

"I'm taking a break. Having a coffee. Everyone else got one."

"There's no time. Fred, the delivery guy for the Baking Crate orders, will be here any minute. I had to ask him to push our pickup back. We can't be sitting around. We need to get them over to the back door, then we need to clean this place up."

I looked around at the mess of the kitchen—bowls, cookie sheets everywhere. Just then there was a knock on the back door.

"Oh God, he's here," she said, panicking, grabbing one of the carts and pulling it over to the back door.

She pushed the door open, allowing him to step inside. "Sorry, a little behind today," she cried.

"No worries, Melinda. We heard what happened to Brooke. I'm sure you're doing your best, so if you need some pickup adjustments, just let me know," he said, smiling at her.

"Tristan. Bring those over here!" she yelled.

I got up, first taking another sip of coffee, and began pushing the carts over to the door. Fred began grabbing boxes, carefully loading them into his truck, and as soon as all the carts were empty, he closed the doors to his truck and wished us a good day. As we shut the back door, we both turned to look at the mess we still had to clean up.

Immediately, Melinda began washing, while I took the sheets of parchment off each of the cookie trays and began putting them back where I'd gotten them from.

"What are you doing? You know those trays need to be washed right."

"Oh yes, of course. I'll load them in once I'm finished," I lied.

Melinda worked circles around me, washing and cleaning up everything, and soon she stood at the back door, her coat and purse in hand. "Finish loading those trays and make sure you unload them tonight," she instructed.

"Sure thing."

"Be ready tomorrow because we do it all again," she sang.

"What do you mean?"

"Well, the Baking Crate orders were already up to fifty last I checked, and we have some large tray orders to get ready for the inn."

I swallowed hard. I was already exhausted and it had been one day. I had no idea what it was going to be like tomorrow, since today had been one of the worst days of my life. I turned to the machine I was loading the trays in to be washed and continued on while Melinda walked out the back door.

Brooke

❦

IT HAD BEEN three days since Tristan had been here. Three entire days of The Crispy Biscuit being run by one person I trusted immensely and one that I wouldn't trust to with even a small remedial task.

I'd watched the traffic come and go. Everyone in Willow Valley was gearing up for Christmas. Parties, family dinners, and client appreciation gifts should be flying out the door every single second, and it was killing me that I had absolutely no idea what condition they were leaving in. I knew I could trust Melinda. I had taught her my style of care and perfection. Tristan, however, was another story.

I sat with my computer in front of me, trying to figure out how to get back to work without the worry of crutches. They were just too slippery to be used on a floor that was covered in flour. I'd opened the browser to a company that sold knee scooters. I watched a couple of videos and decided that this was my answer. I pulled out my credit card and input the information and hit purchase. There was no way I could continue to sit over here panicking.

I grabbed the bottle of wine Tristan had pulled out for me and poured more into my glass, then I pulled the blanket off the back of the chair and threw it over my legs, reclining back. I grabbed my book and began reading where I'd left off. Tristan had gone over to the inn to see his boss. He said they were having a meeting before the contest and he had to turn in a couple of articles he'd been working on, so I finally had some time to myself.

I had just gotten into the book when the phone let out a shrill ring.

"Hello," I said into the receiver.

"Hey it's me. How is it going?" Melinda asked.

"Well, I'm going to go crazy," I cried. "How did it go today?" I prayed that it had gone better than I feared.

"Oh, it was...shall we say interesting." Melinda giggled.

"What happened now?" Melinda had sent me a text after the first day Tristan had worked with her telling me all about the chocolate chip cookie disaster, and every single disaster after that.

"It's almost as if the guy has no regard for the work he

does. I'm shocked he's been able to hold a job as long as he has at *Festive Treasures*," Melinda said.

"I told you." I laughed. I had no idea why I was laughing. There was nothing about my situation that was funny.

"I know you did. Although, he does have one thing going for him: he is kinda cute." Melinda giggled.

It was sad to say but she was right, he was cute. However, his looks were all Tristan had going for him. "I can say the first time I ran into him I thought he was good looking, until he spoke, that is." We both laughed.

"Honestly, Brooke, he is trying to help. I've just been giving him small jobs that I don't have time for. I've been doing all the baking. He's been the one boxing the orders, but I've checked them all."

"Well, thank God for you doing all the baking. At least I know the people are getting the treats they are used to." I giggled.

"Seriously though, maybe you need to give the guy a bit of a break. He is stepping up."

I thought for a second. My only issue was I didn't know why he was stepping up. He literally owed me nothing, and well, I just had a sinking feeling he wasn't doing it because he felt bad.

"He's been good to you, right?"

"Yes, he has. He's made sure that all my needs are taken care of."

"See, give him a bit of a break. Put some faith into the situation."

I couldn't help but giggle. "Oh are you saying I should give him a break by tripping him."

"Brooke! No! The way your luck is, you'd end up getting nabbed for assault or something." Melinda laughed.

"Yeah, you're probably right. He's actually lucky that I'm not suing him over this!"

"Well, you can't sue over an accident."

I grew quiet, thinking of the competition coming up. I had no idea how I was going to enter that now. I wouldn't be able to hobble up the stairs. I let out a sigh.

"What is it?"

"Oh I was just thinking of the competition, how I am going to have to let the dream of getting first place go for this year. It's just not going to be possible."

"Oh no, we will make it happen. Don't you worry. I've been practicing and I've almost perfected that recipe. I've been making small batches of those cinnamon buns all week, and both Trinity and Peggy were in yesterday and they had one. They said they are almost as good as the ones you made. Oh, and they send their regards, told you to get better soon!"

"Yeah, I'm sure I'm the talk of the town right about now."

"Honestly, well, yes, you are. But their thoughts are

with you, and they wish you a speedy recovery. They are all excited to see that you are healed up and back at work soon." Melinda giggled.

"Oh have you been able to keep up with all the Baking Crate orders?"

Melinda let out a bit of a sigh. "Yeah, they are coming in fast and furious now though. I think more than last year, from what I remember."

"I figured they would be. I haven't gone in to check anything because I know me, I won't be able to sit here if I do. However, the good news is I ordered a knee scooter. I haven't said anything to Tristan yet, but I'll be back at work once it arrives."

"I'm not gonna lie, I'm happy that you ordered one." Melinda giggled.

"Listen I'm going to let you go. Get some rest," I said as I heard the key in the lock. I didn't want Tristan to think that I was checking up on him.

"Have a good night, and do your best not to drool over that god you've got living in your house."

"Please, once you know him better, or if I told you a bunch of things from school, you'll be looking at him way differently," I whispered, while the thought of him standing shirtless in my bedroom the other night invaded my memory.

"Night, Brooke."

I hung up the phone just as the door flew open.

Tristan stood there, bundled in a winter coat, carrying a tray of pizza. He closed the door behind him and smiled. "Hey."

"Hi, how did everything go?" I asked.

"Fine, just fine. I figured you might be hungry, so I stopped off at a small pizzeria joint. Pepperoni, mushroom, and pineapple."

I crinkled my nose. "Well, I was good...up until the pineapple part!" I exclaimed.

"Come on, Brooke, tell me you like pineapple."

"Oh I do, just not on pizza, but I am starving, so I'll just pick it off."

Tristan shook his head as he placed the box down on the table and took off his coat. Then he went into the kitchen and returned with two plates and some napkins. I watched as he lifted the lid and pulled two slices out and handed me the plate.

"Thanks."

He grabbed two for himself and then sat down on the couch.

It was well after midnight. The house was quiet, the front room dark, and I lay in bed, once again, staring up at the ceiling. Tristan had run me a hot bath after we'd eaten; he'd even gone to the trouble of lighting a few candles and adding some bubble bath, which had shocked me. Then he'd helped me into the bathroom, returned with my book, and left me to get into the bath on my own. Once I'd dried off and changed into my pajamas, he'd come in and helped get me to the bed.

So much of me wanted to hate him, and part of me still did, but now that he was showing a human side to himself, he was becoming more likable.

I let out a breath and rolled onto my side. The wind was blowing and howling fiercely outside. Willow Valley was in line of some horrible winter storms this week and it looked like we were indeed going to get them.

I'd just closed my eyes when my phone gently vibrated against my nightstand. I reached for it and saw a message from Trinity.

TRINITY: Brooke check this out...I think you should be aware of it.

There was a link following her words, so I clicked on it. As I watched the video that had been posted to YouTube, I wanted to die. It was the day of the tryouts, and it showed exactly what had happened. I watched with horror as I saw Tristan stick his legs out just as I went to walk by him. He had done this on purpose. Anger raced through me as I watched it again and again.

When I could no longer take it, I shut it off and rolled

over onto my back in a huff. Accident. It had been an accident, he said. Didn't look like one to me. I wanted to scream, but instead tears slipped from my eyes. I clenched my fists as my body tensed.

I grabbed my phone and was about to put it back when it vibrated again. This time it was an email from my contact at Baking Crate. I frowned. Melinda said they had gotten every single order out on time.

I opened the email and my eyes nearly fell out of their sockets. Ten customer complaints had been sent in due to improper packaging. I noticed there were image attachments, so I clicked on them, each one producing a photo of broken cookies and opened boxes inside of the larger box. As I studied the images, I noticed that there was nowhere near enough packing paper put inside to secure the boxes. Melinda had said she had checked every one.

Then I went back to the email and read through it. My stomach turned as I read the last paragraph. Due to issues with packaging and the fact that so many had come in all at once, they were threatening to close my Baking Crate account.

My eyes burnt and the words blurred as I tried to focus and fight off tears at the same time. I knew I should have just shut down and closed the store, or at least let Baking Crate know of the incident so they could close down the online portion for now.

I shut off my phone, completely heartbroken, and lay

in the dark. I rolled onto my side and allowed the tears to fall. I prayed that my knee scooter arrived in the morning and that I could fix everything that had been done. I'd immediately start by replacing those orders that had arrived damaged free of charge.

Tristan

It had been one hell of a morning. We'd fallen behind, and weren't ready to get those orders ready for pickup in time. We'd asked Fred for an extension on our pickup, but he wasn't able to help us today, so instead I thought I'd drive them over. I now sat outside of the Willow Valley Post Office and cut the engine.

I pulled the door open and stepped inside, waiting my turn. I didn't have to wait long as Fred spotted me right away and came over.

"Hey, Tristan! I can come and help you out," he said. "I'll just grab a cart from the back, and we can get them loaded onto the truck. You're just on time. Any later and they wouldn't be going out until tomorrow."

I turned and made my way out front and opened the

trunk just as he appeared from the side of the building pulling a cart. Together we loaded box upon box onto the cart, then I closed the trunk.

"Just wait. There are a couple more on the back seat."

"No problem. I can't believe how many packages Brooke is sending out these days. It's crazy. I remember when this first started. I think her first week she sent out ten packages in total."

"Wow, really?" I questioned.

"Yeah she has really built something for herself. We are all so proud of her," Fred said, taking the last couple of packages from me.

"I'm glad things are going well for her," I muttered. "That's all of them." I closed the back door.

"Looks like her hard work has paid off. I'll be coming in with the wife on Saturday for breakfast. Let Brooke know we'll also be ordering our usual Christmas Eve tray. She'll know what I'm talking about."

"Will do," I said, watching as he took the cart back to the back of the building.

He turned and waved before disappearing. I was about to walk to the other side of the car when two people walking by smiled and said hello. "See you tomorrow morning, Tristan," they sang.

I'd started helping Melinda at the counter when things got busy, and I'd recognized them from yesterday morning. They'd both come in for a hot chocolate. Was this what it was like to live in a small town? This certainly didn't happen in the city, no one cared about who you were or what you did. You just went to work, got your groceries, and existed within your own little bubble. Here was different. I could understand why Brooke loved her community so much. These people actually cared about one another. It had shocked me how many people had asked about her over the last few days and wished her well. Hell, when I'd torn my rotator cuff playing ball, only one person in the office had asked how I was doing; the rest were too busy attending to their own problems and their own lives.

"Yep, tomorrow!" I called back and then headed around to the driver's side and climbed in the car.

I made my way back to the bakery and pulled up to the curb just in time to see Melinda standing on the sidewalk.

"Hey, thanks for letting me borrow your car," I said, handing her the keys. "Don't think they would have fit in mine."

"No problem. I have to run. I have a doctor's appointment. Cici is just closing up. There are a few more dishes to do, but nothing you can't handle, right?"

"Nope. I got it. Have a good night."

Just then the front door opened and Cici appeared,

locking the front door. "Good night, guys." She waved as she headed off down the street.

"Back door is still open. Make sure you set the alarm before you leave," Cici called out.

I watched as she climbed into the car and took off. I walked back to the back door and pulled it open. I made my way across the kitchen and went to turn lights on when I heard a tiny whimper, followed by another one, then a sniffle.

"Hello?" I called.

"What?" a sobbing voice called back.

I went around the corner and saw Brooke standing at the sink, her knee propped up on a scooter, her back turned away from me.

"Tristan, what are you doing here?" she cried.

I looked around at the small mess that was still left to clean up. "I came in to finish cleaning. However, I think that question should be asked of you."

"No, I mean what are you even doing here? Are you trying to destroy everything I've worked so hard for?" She sniffled.

"Why would you think that?"

She repeated my question under in her breath in a mocking tone. I couldn't help but frown. Was she having some sort of breakdown?

"Why would you think that?" I repeated.

"Well, I've lost the contest because of my ankle."

"You haven't lost the contest. It hasn't happened yet, and I've told you the ankle was an accident."

"Really? Are you sure about that?" She turned and looked at me, her eyes full of anger.

I didn't know what she was referring to, but I had not tripped her on purpose, that much I knew. "Yes, I'm sure."

"Well, it sure looked like it was on purpose. I watched the entire thing, from about fifteen different angles online. Just look..." She reached into her pocket and shoved her phone at me.

I took the phone from her small hand and watched the screen. There it was. I had relaxed back and crossed my legs out in front of me just as she went to walk across the stage. She was right; from watching this, it certainly looked like I had done it on purpose. Her eyes were fixed ahead of her, a smile on her face, and then there were cookies everywhere and she was on the ground.

"Well, of course, this looks that way..." I said, swallowing hard, staring at the screen until she pulled the phone from my hand.

"Well if that isn't enough to prove it to you, all you need to do is watch the fourteen other videos. Honestly, I should sue you for damages."

I looked at her, praying to God she didn't go down that road. I had nothing—absolutely nothing. It would be pointless for her to do that.

"Then there is this," she said, shoving the phone back from me.

I stood there, not saying anything, waiting for her to show me the next thing.

"Here." She shoved the phone at me again.

I looked at the screen and the picture of messed-up boxes of cookies. "What's that?" I questioned.

"What's that?" she questioned in a mocking tone. "These are the orders that were sent out to customers. They are a complete disaster!" she cried.

"Well, surely, you aren't blaming me for this?"

She glared at me. "Who do you think I'm going to blame?"

"The post office." I shrugged and gave her a cocky grin, certain that she would move the blame from me to the postal service.

"Right, yes, what on earth was I thinking. I've only been doing this longer than a year, every order arriving in perfect shape, until now, and I am suddenly going to blame the post office!" she yelled, pocketing her phone.

"Well, I don't see how you can blame me."

"You do realize that I've spoken to Melinda. I know you're the one who packs the boxes—every single box. I also know that you have not followed any one of the directions in my book, which is the least you could do."

"I thought they were... more of a guideline."

Brooke just stood there, staring at me. "You know,

Tristan, you don't run a bakery. In fact, I have no idea what it is you have done in your life. I don't even know if you actually graduated school or not, but I do know that you clearly are not qualified to work in this kind of environment. You may as well just leave, if this is all the help you're going to be."

I didn't know what to say. Was she kicking me out? I stood there, just looking back at her, at her beautiful eyes. God she was even more gorgeous when she was angry.

"I can do better," I said in a low voice, praying that she didn't want me to really leave. I had nowhere to go. My credit card had been frozen due to non-payment, and my account was almost at its max. Vicki was still angry as hell at me, even more so since the video from the other day had gotten leaked. I was shocked she hadn't fired me yet.

"Can you? Can you really? I don't know if you know what it takes to get an account with Baking Crate, but I will say that they don't let just anyone have one. It takes years of proving yourself, years of applying."

I nodded. "Yes, I know. I was somewhat shocked to see you had one, actually. There are much bigger establishments that don't have an account."

"That's right, and now because of you, they are threatening to close mine."

I looked at her, shock lining my face. "Because of five little wrecked orders?" I asked.

"Ten."

"Still…it was only ten."

"Yes, it was only ten. However, it was ten in the same day. So, as per their contract, my account may be closed because of ten little orders. Luckily for me, they know my work, so they are considering overlooking it."

"Wow…"

Brooke stood there, frowning at me. I had no idea that they were that strict. Yet I felt they were overreacting a little bit.

"Wow what?" she asked, her intense eyes, never leaving mine.

"Perhaps they should understand that shit happens when you ship things." I shrugged.

I could see the fire in her eyes. The tears were now gone. She wheeled her scooter an inch toward me and continued as she spoke.

"You know, I remember you back in school. No regard for anything you did. It was fine then, but this? This is my livelihood. This is how I pay my bills, my mortgage, for my car, buy my food. This isn't just a little side project I have going. I know you probably don't care, but you have no idea how hard I've worked to accomplish what I've done, nor do you know what I've had to give up to get what I have. I have employees who count on a paycheck to look after their families. You're not messing with a grade this time," she said, poking me hard in the chest with her index finger.

"I know that."

"Do you? Do you actually understand that? Do you actually understand that if my Baking Crate account gets closed down that my life will be impacted and so will the others?"

"Yes, of course, I do."

"Then smarten the hell up or leave." Immediately, she pinched the bridge of her nose and shut her eyes tight. "I've got a headache. I've got to get out of here!" she yelled, wheeling her way across the kitchen.

I wanted to call out to her, to apologize. I hadn't quite grasped exactly how hard it had been for her to build this place. How could I? I also hadn't truly grasped what this place meant to her, how important it was.

I jumped as the back door slammed shut, then I took a look around at the small pile of dishes that were in the sink and over to the cookies trays I'd been told to wash for the past few days and hung my head.

I thought about Melinda, how kind she'd been to me, even though I'd probably been nothing more than a pain in her ass. Then I thought about Cici. We hadn't worked together much, but she seemed like she was a sweet girl. Then I thought about one of the prep cooks who had shared the fact that her brother was ill and she was working only to help with medical expenses. All those people counted on Brooke, and here I was not giving a single fuck about anything I did.

I sat down on the chair I normally used to have my coffee and looked at the book Brooke had given me. When I originally looked at it, I'd skimmed through it, rolling my eyes at every single thing that she'd written. I'd purposely not packed those boxes tight enough because I hadn't cared enough. Then my brother's words floated through my mind, how I didn't care about anyone but myself, and that someday when it would really matter, it would catch up to me. He'd been right. This entire time, I'd been here helping her for one reason. I'd been praying that she didn't go after the magazine or me. It was about damage control to protect only one person, and that was me.

Something had to change.

I flipped the light on and began loading all the cookie trays into the machine one by one. Then I ran and got the book Brooke had given me and flipped it to the cleaning chapter. I followed the directions to set the machine, then I went over to the sink and began washing all that was there.

After that, I made the solution to mop the floor and took my time cleaning every single corner, under racks and out into the storefront. These things had all been my responsibility, and I'd half-assed it just like I normally would in my own life.

Then I went over to the printer and pulled off all the orders that had come through online. I set them all out and grabbed some paper and a pencil and began marking down all the cookies we'd need to fill the boxes, along with amounts.

I planned to make this right. I had to. It was no longer about protecting me. Now it was about protecting her and her employees. I had to prove to her that I actually cared, and that was going to start right now.

Brooke

WHEN I'D GOTTEN HOME, I popped two headache pills and heated up some soup I'd had in the freezer. I was angry and frustrated with myself that I'd allowed myself to think Tristan had changed. My body ached as I put in a load of laundry and sat down with my soup and a bottle of wine in front of the TV. I flipped the channels until I came to some silly cheesy Christmas movie. I let out a sigh and broke some crackers up into my soup. I literally felt that I was living one of these silly movies, only I feared that my ending wasn't going to turn out as well as it did for the characters.

Once I'd eaten my soup, I flipped the fireplace on. It was cold and snowy out, and I just wanted to be warm and comfortable and get lost in my oversized comfy couch. I grabbed the blanket that I kept on the back of the couch and threw it over myself, and then I arranged the pillows and relaxed against them. It took time but eventually my body to begin to relax.

I blinked. The room was dark. I had no idea where I was, so I sat up and looked around the familiar room. How had I gotten into my bedroom, I wondered. I didn't remember coming to bed, yet here I was, tucked under the covers. Kicking the covers off me, I looked down to see I was in my pajamas. Last I remembered, I was in my sweats.

I grabbed my knee scooter and made my way into the bathroom. I took a few minutes to put my hair up and get dressed. As I approached the bedroom door, I noticed my sweats were laying on the small chair just inside my door. I let out a sigh and noticed that the lights were not on yet in the other room, and I glanced to the clock. It was only four.

I quietly opened the door and rolled out into the living room where Tristan was sound asleep on the couch. I stood there, not wanting to wake him, and just watched him. He slept shirtless; the blankets stopped at his waste. I took in his broad shoulders, chiseled chest, and abs. Then I looked up to his face. He had a darker complexion and very chiseled features. I actually found him more hand-some now than I did when we were younger. It was too bad that everything changed when he opened his mouth, I thought to myself as I looked at his full, bowed lips.

I quietly wheeled myself into the kitchen and turned

the kettle on. I didn't want to be caught staring at him if he woke up. I pulled a mug from the cupboard, along with a teabag, and stood waiting for it to boil and popped a bagel into the toaster. I looked out the kitchen window. A fresh blanket of snow lay in the driveway, and it looked deep. It would be a challenge getting this scooter through that, I thought to myself, hoping I would be able to get over there before Tristan woke up.

I'd just sat down and taken a bite of my bagel when Tristan appeared in the doorway. I'd only turned on the small light over the stove, so he probably wasn't expecting me to be there. He stood there, his hair a mess, running his hand over his face, in nothing but boxers. I could see the outline of his semi-hard cock and couldn't help but take in his flexed abs as he stretched.

With my hand holding the bagel to my mouth, I felt like I was completely frozen at the sight in front of me. As his eyes met mine, I prayed I wasn't drooling.

"Good morning," he said, coming into the kitchen and going over to the cupboard to pull out his own mug along with the instant coffee.

I didn't answer him. I just sat there staring. What the hell was wrong with me all of a sudden? It was as if one look at him like this was enough to erase all that he'd done. I swallowed hard and tore my eyes away from him. "Morning," I said, taking a bite of my bagel.

"Sleep well?" he questioned.

"Yeah, about that..." I said, almost choking on the food that had been in my mouth. "I um, don't remember going to bed."

He chuckled. "That's because you didn't. I stayed at the bakery late, preparing for today," he said, bringing his coffee over to the table and sitting down across from me. "When I got back, you were sound asleep on the couch. So I got you ready for bed."

Horrified, I looked at him. "You did what?"

"Relax, it's not like I haven't seen a naked woman before." There was that cocky grin again.

My mouth dropped at his words, and suddenly, I wanted to die. Not because he had seen me naked, but because I'd remembered getting dressed yesterday morning and my bra and panties hadn't matched. *They were supposed to match weren't they?*

"Although, I will say, I've never seen a grown woman with little pink bunnies on her panties before," he said as he took a sip. "Puppy dog Christmas pajamas, bunny panties, what other animal attire you have in that drawer?"

I had never wanted to curl up in a hole and die as badly as I did right now. I'd been slumming it for a couple of days, and the one day that I just pulled whatever out of the drawer to put under my yoga pants had been the day I'd decided to drink a bottle of wine and pass out.

"It was sort of cute. Kind of turned me on a little." He winked.

"Just stop talking," I gritted, hiding my red cheeks behind my hands.

"There's nothing to embarrassed about." He chuckled. "You are an attractive woman."

"I'm not embarrassed. I'm...I'm..."

"Oh? You're not? Because the red cheeks say otherwise?"

"No, I'm irritated. Now if you'll excuse me, I have to get over there," I said, getting up from the table, wishing that he wasn't watching my every move.

"I'll be over shortly. I'm just gonna take a shower."

"You do whatever you need to do."

"In that case, I may be a little late!"

"Why on earth would you be late? You have plenty of time," I said, reaching for my scooter.

"I like to take my time when I relieve some tension."

My head spun so fast I feared I'd get whiplash. One look at his face and I could feel the heat running through my body.

"And you're blushing again." He chuckled, reaching over to my plate and taking a bite of my bagel.

"I'm leaving now," I said, scooting out of the room as fast as I could. I'd never been so happy to have the cold morning air hit my face as I was today. I'd been on fire in that kitchen, and I'd wanted to die at the thought of him seeing me naked.

I was shocked to find that Tristan had cleaned the entire place top to bottom and had gotten everything organized for baking this morning. I'd quickly looked over everything and was surprised to find that each order had been accounted for and had been perfectly batched together by recipe. I'd stopped in my tracks when I went to head to the pantry to find that he had even baked all the Grinch Crinkle Cookies, and he'd even made extras to put out in the display.

I took one of the cookies from the cooling rack and popped it into my mouth. They tasted exactly like mine, and as I chewed it, tears came to my eyes. I was about to grab another one when I heard the back door open and close and heard voices. I quickly made my way into the pantry.

"Morning," I heard Melinda call.

"I know she came over here," I heard Tristan say.

"Perhaps she's in her office. I'll go check."

I wiped my eyes. Had he really done all that? I wiped my cheeks again and grabbed a couple of bottles from the shelf that I'd need and placed them in the small basket I'd tied to the front of my scooter and made my way out into the kitchen. "Morning," I called.

The three of us got right to work, and I watched as Tristan grabbed my notebook and went about following another one of the recipes I'd written out. He first calculated the amount of ingredients he needed and went about his work as if he'd worked with me for years. Melinda looked at me quizzially. I shrugged. I'd not told her about the blowup I'd had, nor had I told her about the incident with Baking Crate. I'd just kept that to myself. I didn't want her to feel like it was her fault.

Soon we were open. Cici and Melinda waited on tables for the breakfast rush, while Tristan and I worked side-by-side baking everything. When it would get busy, he'd take time going out to the counter and serving customers. I watched through the small window in the door and was surprised to see him smiling and joking with the customers. It was as if something had changed overnight, and I was living in some alternate universe.

I'd just popped the last of the cookies on the trays for the display cases and had to take a seat; my foot was throbbing, even though I'd done nothing but rest it on my scooter. I poured a mug of apple cider and had just sat down and placed my booted foot on the chair in front of me when Tristan came back in.

"It's finally settling down out there," he said, coming over and leaning against the table.

"Yeah, it normally slows after the breakfast rush,

thankfully. In here is a different story, however. Seventy-five packages to go out today."

"Seventy-five? I thought it was sixty-five," Tristan replied.

"Well, I'm replacing the ten to the people who complained. It was the only way to get them to remove the strikes from my account." I shrugged. "My foot is killing me," I said, reaching down and rubbing the outside of the boot as if it were going to help.

"You just rest. I'll pack them up."

I watched as he moved over to the packing table and began setting up boxes. Then he moved the orders, one by one, and placed them down in front of each of the boxes as I'd instructed. He placed each of the items neatly inside the boxes, arranging them exactly how I'd instructed, then he wrapped each tray and placed it inside the boxes, closing them and placing my Crispy Biscuit sticker exactly how I'd of done it. I watched as he placed each of the boxes of cookies inside the Baking Crate boxes, shoving packing paper around my smaller boxes, adding more of the crinkle paper to make sure they were packed securely before sealing the boxes shut and placing the labels on them.

I was so surprised that he was taking this seriously I had to check my forehead to see if I had a fever. Then I picked up my mug and took a sip and continued watching him. I was floored to watch him in action. He actually could do a good job if he put his mind to it, I thought to myself. I finished my apple cider and had gotten up once the pain medication had taken effect and helped finish packing the last of the orders.

Soon we were laughing and talking, instead of fighting, and it was as if we'd always gotten along. Together we loaded all boxes onto the cart just in time to see Fred pull in.

"Just in time," I said, excited that we'd pulled it off.

"Yep, just in time," he said, meeting my eyes.

I softly smiled at him. "Thank you," I whispered, trying not to get choked up.

He had no idea how much it meant to me that he'd actually cared enough to take what I'd said seriously, but he had done it. I had to stop a couple of times as we worked together to help load the orders. I watched with how he interacted with Fred, speaking as if they too were old friends. They talked, joked, and Tristan even offered to help Fred with a chore at his place. As I handed one of the last two boxes to Fred, he stopped and cleared his throat.

"Brooke, Ava wanted to know if you'd gotten your Christmas tree yet?"

I shook my head. "No, unfortunately, I haven't. I probably won't be having the ladies over for the holiday party either. With this foot like this, I'm barely able to get around." I smiled, trying to hide my disappointment.

"Oh, my dear, Ava will be disappointed, but I know

she will understand. She always loves getting out with you girls."

Ava had been my mother's best friend growing up. I'd often invited her over during the holidays, since my own mother was off on her own adventures. She loved sitting and looking at my tree and every year she begged me for decorating tips. However, with all these changes, it didn't even feel like Christmas.

"Let her know I'll have her over for coffee and some sinful desserts though. It just won't be with the usual atmosphere." As the words left my mouth, I saw Tristan out the corner of my eyes watching me, an odd look on his face.

Fred loaded the last two boxes in the back of the van and gave me a hug, then shook hands with Tristan, firming up the plans they'd made. Then he made his way to the driver's seat, climbed in, and waved good-bye, pulling out of the driveway.

"Well, that was a super productive day," Tristan said, looking around at the mess we had yet to clean up.

"Yes, it was," I answered.

Cici and Melinda came into the kitchen, both of them giggling to themselves, and took a look around at the mess.

"Everything all closed up?" I questioned.

"Yep," they said in unison, moving over to the sinks where they began washing things.

"Brooke, can I see you for a moment?" Tristan asked.

I looked over to him and nodded, getting up off the chair I was sitting in and moving over to him with my scooter.

"What's up?" I questioned, looking into his blue eyes.

"You look exhausted. Why don't you and the girls take off, and I'll get this place cleaned up. Then I'll cook you dinner."

I did my best not to look at him skeptically, and looked over to the two girls who'd both been working their asses off to help me in my time of need. It was the beginning of December, and I was sure they both had shopping to do. I nodded my head in silent agreement.

"Okay, if you're sure you can..."

"I can handle it," he said, placing his large hands on my shoulders. "Trust me."

I had no choice but to trust him at this point. He'd proven himself today, and I felt that if I didn't give him the benefit of the doubt now, then it would be like I was saying he hadn't tried, which he had, and he'd succeeded. I was actually proud of him.

I yelled out to the girls, giving them both the word that they could leave early. They looked at me, grinning, and before I knew what had flown past me, they were out the door on the way to do some shopping together. I waited until they'd both gone out of sight to head back home and leave Tristan to prove himself to me once again.

Tristan

I STOOD at the stove stirring my signature pasta sauce, while the meatballs I'd made roasted in the oven. Brooke sat at the small kitchen table, a glass of wine in front of her, flipping through a holiday magazine.

"I'm not going to lie, I'm starving," Brooke said as I grated the cheese I needed for the garlic bread I was making.

I'd gone to the small grocery store once I'd been finished cleaning and had gotten all the ingredients for dinner.

"I think you're going to love this, honestly."

I stirred the sauce and checked the meatballs to find that they were finished, so I pulled them from the oven, setting them over on a cooling rack, before salting the pasta water and dumping in the pasta I'd bought, giving it a quick stir.

"So, I bet you miss not owning a restaurant?" Brooke asked.

I froze at her question. I couldn't fabricate a story this time. Instead, I shook my head. "I never ended up making it happen." I swallowed hard, concentrating on making sure the garlic bread was perfectly seasoned.

"Oh? I figured that was why you didn't return to school."

I thought back to that time, to how horrible it had been for me. "Unfortunately not."

"What happened?" she questioned.

I thought back to that time, remembering exactly how things had gone.

I opened the door to the house and stepped inside. It was quiet as I placed my bags down on the floor just inside the door. Both of my parents' cars were outside in the driveway so I knew they were home. I poked my head into the sitting room to find it empty. I moved to the kitchen, but both the butler and cook were nowhere to be found. I frowned.

"Hello," I called.

When no one answered, I made my way down the hall toward my father's office. The closer I got, I could hear voices, and so I just stood outside the open door, listening.

"I don't see how much longer we can go on paying for them, Lenore," my father said in a comforting tone. "The company is almost bankrupt, and—"

"Oh my God, Frank, what are we going to do? How are we going to pay for this house and our lifestyles?" my mother cried.

"Well, thankfully, the house is paid for. The rest of it, well, I am sure I can rebuild. I should have made sufficient changes when things turned. Instead, I tried to keep my employees happy by giving them raises. I kept spending, thinking it would change things. It never should have happened. I should have been smarter, especially when I knew we were in the negative."

"What about our staff?" she cried.

"Well, for now, we will only need them during special occasions, until things turn around, then we will call them all back."

What the hell was going on? I wondered. Just then, Mom began to cry. I had to step away. I didn't want to hear her cry. I made my way back down the hall and picked up my bags and quietly made my way out the front door.

Three hours later, I returned home. I hadn't told my parents I was coming home for the summer. They thought I would be staying in the dorms. I walked up the staircase and slid my key into the lock.

"Tristan, you're home!" Mom said, coming out of the sitting room.

I put my bags down and welcomed the hug she wanted to give me. "Hey, Mom. I hope it's okay that I came home."

"Of course. Your father is in the office. He will be happy to see you," she said, making her way in that direction.

"Don't bother him. It's okay," I said, trying to stop her, but she continued toward the back of the house. "Take a seat. We will be right out," she called back.

I wandered into the sitting room and looked around. I noticed the pillows on the couch were out of place, and there were a couple of glasses on the table. There was a fine layer of dust on a couple of the tables that lined the wall, and I suddenly wondered how long they had been without their house staff.

"Tristan, welcome home," my father's deep voice rang through the room. "Take a seat. We want to talk to you about something."

I looked at my parents, already knowing what was coming, since I'd eavesdropped earlier, and sat down.

"Tristan, we have some news we want to share with you."

"Okay," I said, sitting down and looking at them.

"We've had to let some of our personal staff go, son. Things are not good financially." He lowered his eyes to the

ground, probably ashamed of himself and what had happened.

"What happened?" I asked, shocked at what my father was saying.

"The markets took a turn for the worse, business has slowed down, and honestly, the profits have been non-existent for about three years."

"I see," I muttered, not believing what I was hearing.

"It's a tremendously stressful time here at the moment, but we are trying to work our way through it."

"What can I do to help?" I questioned.

"Nothing, son. Just keep your head down and do your best at school. The only part I'm thankful for is the fact that your schooling is completely paid for."

I thought back to the money my father had given me for school. He'd paid for my tuition in full; however, I had taken the second semester tuition and, instead of paying for school, I had used it to live my life. I had purchased new furniture for the dorm room instead of using what was already there because it hadn't been good enough. I'd spent it drinking and partying with friends and had nothing left to show for it because I figured that when I needed more, I'd just call and get some. Perhaps my brother had been right, and I needed to take my life a little more seriously.

"I'll um, get a student loan," I said without thinking, looking up at my parents. "Please don't worry about me having to return to school and paying for anything."

"*No, you won't. That will only bring attention to our situation and point to money trouble for us in the eyes of our friends and colleagues. You're school has been paid for in full. You don't need to worry.*"

I swallowed hard and was about to say something when Dad cleared his throat.

"*We don't want our reputations ruined in the eyes of this. We will make due and we will be back stronger than ever in no time. For now, the staff have been dismissed. They will be called back for the big functions we have scheduled for the summer, and hopefully come fall things will have turned around.*"

Only things got worse as summer progressed. Dad eventually had to close the doors on his company, all major events they'd planned had to be canceled, and soon we were faced with a for sale sign every time we had to pull into the driveway.

I stopped at the end of the driveway to get the mail but found the mailbox empty and pulled through the gates and up the drive. I opened the door to the house and stepped inside to see my father come out of the sitting room, holding a letter in his hand, the look on his face one I'd never seen before.

"*Hey, Dad, something wrong?*"

He gave me a stern look and shook his head. "*Come in here for a moment, would you?*" *he barked.*

I stepped into the sitting room. My mother sat on the

couch, her face in her hands, her shoulders shaking. My father stood with his back toward me. I stood there not sure what to do.

"What's wrong?" I asked, worried that perhaps Mom was sick.

"Take a seat," my father barked.

I lowered myself down onto the over-sized chair and waited. My father stood there holding a piece of paper as my mother let out another sob.

"Do you mind telling me—" I started.

"Do I mind telling you what? How you stole the money I gave you to pay for two years' tuition, for two separate programs to find out that you only paid for one?"

I froze. I'd told the school I'd pay them when I returned. I had no clue how my father had found out. "I uh, I don't know what you are talking about?" I lied.

"Do you not think that the school was going to come to me for the remainder of your tuition?" He waved the letter he held in his hand in the air.

I didn't know what to say as I stared at the piece of paper.

"Well?" my father barked as my mom continued to cry.

"I just…"

"You just figured you would get more money. Isn't that right. I hold an endless supply don't I."

The air grew thick, and it was hard for me to swallow. I

hated listening to my mother cry, and even more I hated my father when he was angry.

"Where did we go wrong, son?"

"You didn't," I bit out, feeling sick to my stomach as my mother sobbed.

"Well, I must have. Never in my life did I figure I couldn't trust you with money. I guess I should have treated you like the child you are and just paid for the tuition myself," Dad bit out.

"Dad I—"

"You know, I've never understood why you can't be more like your brother," Dad said. "He's never once came to me for money. Never once. He paid for his own schooling, then went off and staked his own claim."

"I'm not my brother!" I yelled.

"Damn right you're not. You'll have to come up with your tuition for this year. We can't do it," Dad said, dropping the letter to the floor as he made his way over to my mother, who sat there, her shoulders shaking as she sobbed into her hands. He placed his hands on her shoulders, trying to comfort her.

"Mom, I'm sorry," I cried. "Please, let me explain."

Just then Zach stepped into the sitting room. He was the last person I wanted to see—their perfect son. He bent down and picked up the letter my father had dropped and read it over, his eyes meeting mine. He had known that Dad had paid the entire two years' tuition upfront because I'd told him.

"What have you done now?" he asked, looking at our parents and then to me. No doubt he already knew about their financial situation.

"Well, I'm not you, that's what I've done," I bit out.

Zach shook his head, then looked down to the letter he held and back to me. "It's time you grow the hell up, Tristan. That's all I've got to say. Now I think it's time you leave the room," he said, looking to our parents.

I didn't wait. Instead, I stormed out of the room and stopped in the hallway, anger coursing through me as I listened to my brother talk to my parents, offering them help if they needed. He always was the perfect son, and in their eyes could do no wrong. I'd always been the fuckup. I couldn't stand there and listen to them talk anymore. Instead, I ran up the stairs to my bedroom. I flopped down on the bed and placed my arms behind my head and stared up at the ceiling.

I blinked hard. Tears had blurred my eyes at the memory of that summer, and I stood there quietly, not sure I wanted to tell Brooke what had happened. I placed the grated cheese on the bread and then placed them onto a baking screen, switching the oven to broil.

"You don't need to tell me if you don't want to."

"Well, my parents, they lost everything that summer. I just couldn't afford to come back to school. I had to take care of them and make sure that they were okay."

"Oh..."

"Besides, after seeing how much work goes into a small bakery and diner, I'm not really sure I would have lasted in some major restaurant, to be honest. I started work at *Festive Treasures* shortly after that summer. I started as a food critic writing a small column under a pseudonym, and just went from there."

"You would have lasted," she answered. "You'd have put your mind to it, put your soul into it, you would have been fine."

I shook my head. "No, I don't think I would have."

I stirred the pot of sauce, quickly dipping a spoon in to taste. Then dipped it in again and walked over to Brooke, stopping in front of her and blowing on the hot sauce.

"Open up," I said, lowering the spoon and placing it into her mouth.

Her eyes lit up as she tasted the sauce and she softly smiled. "This is excellent."

"You're just saying that." I said, moving across the

kitchen back to the stove where I placed the garlic bread in to cook.

"I'm not, I mean it. It's the best sauce I've tasted," she said, licking her lips.

"Thanks." I grew quiet. No one had ever complimented me before. It felt weird, and I really didn't know what to say or do with it.

"You know, I can see it on your face that you love to cook. You seem to be at peace in the kitchen, even today at the store while baking. It's almost like your soul knows that is the perfect space for you."

I looked over my shoulder at her and smiled. "Thanks, I really do. It's one of the only places I feel like myself is when I am in the kitchen, not necessarily when baking but when cooking."

As the timer went for the oven, I pulled the bubbling cheesy garlic bread from the oven and began plating our food. Then I carried the plates over to the table and set them down, sitting down across from Brooke and filling up both of our glasses with more wine.

"So, what about you?" I asked, digging my fork into the pasta. "Are you happy here, running The Crispy Biscuit?"

She thought for a moment. "You know, I am. I actually wasn't sure I would love it as much as I do. When I was a little girl, I had dreams of growing up and leaving this town and doing something amazing, but the older I got, this was just home. Of course, I wanted to stake my own claim here, but then circumstances changed, and here I am." She smiled softly with a faraway look in her eyes.

"What happened?"

"Well, originally, The Crispy Biscuit was run by my grandmother. My Mom and Dad took it over when she could no longer manage it. I worked there through high school, waiting tables, and when it came time to go to college, I was at a loss. I had no idea what I wanted to do with my life. So, Mom suggested taking a cooking course. I wasn't overly thrilled with the idea, but I did it anyways. I started off here in Willow Valley, doing a couple cooking courses to make sure I liked it first. When I had completed it, I decided to enroll in a professional course.

"Anyways, just before I was leaving for school my grandmother was diagnosed with cancer, and just before she passed away, she told me how proud she was of me for following in the family's footsteps. She was thrilled to know that The Crispy Biscuit would continue on."

I listened with full attention as she spoke. It wasn't a wonder why this place meant so much to her.

"Anyways, time passed and I completed the courses, and a few months after I graduated, my Mom was diagnosed with the exact same cancer. It was a trying time. She had to stop working to go through treatments, and she needed my dad there with her, so they both semi-retired, and I ended up taking over the business on a temporary basis. As time went on, I knew my parents were struggling financially. They were paying for all the travel, and of course, my mom's medical costs. So, I'd decided to help with the cost of those treatments. I took the money from the banked profits of the business, but soon I was having issues paying for things and paying my staff. When my parents found out they, demanded I stop, however, I didn't want to see my parents lose their retirement savings." She swallowed hard and picked up her wine, taking a sip.

"Wow, Brooke, I am so sorry."

"Anyways, one night after a long day, I sat down trying to figure out how I was going to make extra income. The diner took up all my time. There was no way I could pick up another job, so that was when I decided to open up the sweets counter. I'd learned to bake some of the most amazing things at school, and my talent was being wasted by not using it. So, I went to the bank and got a small loan to buy the display cases and I opened that to help pay for my mother's treatments. The diner was running perfectly fine and turning a profit, so I knew I could afford to take my attention from it for a bit to get this going."

"Wow, you did all that for them?"

She nodded her head. "Yes, I did. However, it really was the best decision I ever made. I applied to Baking Crate for seven straight months before they even replied asking for a sample. Once accepted and things got moving, something magical happened. I was able to not only pay for all the things my mom needed, but I was also able to replenish their savings. Then I was able to buy the space next to the diner and add on the extra kitchen space. My mom went through her treatments and recovered, and now they are happily retired," she finished and softly smiled.

"I had no idea..."

"I wouldn't expect you to. No one really does. We kept it quiet. Word spreads in this town fast, in case you didn't find that out when I got hurt, but that is why I fight so hard for this. That part of the business was born entirely because of my want to help my parents. It's my baby, and that is why I am so protective of it. I don't know where I would be without it, or if The Crispy Biscuit would even still be here."

"Wow, Brooke, I truly had no idea." I grew quiet.

"You know what the worst part is?"

I looked at her. She wasn't just running a small-town diner that had a stroke of luck like I'd originally thought. She was running something that literally had been built from the ground up and something that gave the gift of life to another. She'd done all this work for another person. A totally selfless act.

"I don't know if I could do it again if ever I had to," she said, picking up her napkin and dabbing her eyes.

I had no words of advice to give her, probably because

I'd never been in that situation. She wiped her eyes again, took in a breath, then sipped her wine. I watched as she began digging into the food on her plate. As I sat there, the last conversation with my brother popped into my mind. We'd had another one of our famous arguments. As always he was disappointed in me and had no problem expressing that to me. Just before we were about to hang up, he'd told me that he wished I would change and do something for someone else as opposed to always doing things to only benefit myself. Then the only person in my life that I fully admired and still had in my life after my parents' death cleared his throat and told me not to bother calling him again unless I'd changed. The line went dead, and that was the end of our conversation, and that was the last conversation I'd had with my brother. It had been almost three years.

Brooke cleared her throat and met my eyes. "Tristan, this is really, really good. You really should think about opening up a restaurant. I've never tasted anything like this," she said, taking a bite of one of the meatballs on her plate.

"Thanks, but really I know I don't have what it takes. It was just a silly dream."

"No dream is silly. You just need to find a reason inside of yourself to accomplish it, whether it's for yourself or for someone else. You just need to have faith in yourself and your ability." She winked.

An hour later, with all the dishes cleaned and washed, I joined Brooke in the living room. She sat on the couch, her foot out of the boot and elevated. She'd already turned the TV on and a movie was just beginning.

"Care if I join you?" I asked.

"No, of course not," she said, repositioning herself so I could sit down.

I sat beside her, pulling the small ottoman from the foot of her chair so she could elevate her foot easier. Then I grabbed the blanket that was over the back of the chair and fanned it out over Brooke.

"Thank you," she whispered.

"You're welcome," I quietly replied, and placed my arm across the back of the couch and relaxed.

We were halfway through the movie when Brooke stretched and let out a yawn. "You tired? Did you want help to get to bed?" I asked.

"No, I'm okay. Just a little stiff," she said, rubbing her lower back. "Guess that is what happens when you sit around all day."

"You can stretch out if you'd like. I don't bite." I winked. "Well, not unless you want me to."

Brooke rolled her eyes and gave a tiny smile and let out a tiny giggle as she shook her head, "Unbelievable," she whispered under her breath.

"What???"

"Nothing," she said with a smile as she shook her head.

We both grew quiet again and turned our attention back to the television. I leaned back and closed my eyes. I was exhausted after such a long day as well. Next thing I knew, my legs were covered with the blanket I'd gotten for Brooke, and she was curled up into my side, her eyes closed.

I adjusted myself, sinking farther down into the couch, and placed my feet up on the ottoman that she'd been using and rested my arm around her, and together we drifted off while watching the movie.

<h1 style="text-align:center">Brooke</h1>

I slowly opened my eyes, at first not recognizing my surroundings. I wiped my eyes and stretched, then noticed I was on the couch in the living room. The TV had been turned off. The small nightlight that was plugged into the wall in the corner gave off just enough light to be able to see everything.

I hadn't remembered falling asleep. I went to adjust the blankets, but something was stopping them, then I noticed his hand resting on my abdomen. I was about to sit up and go to my bed when I realized just how nice it was to be curled into him. I was warm, and he was snuggly. So, instead of getting up, I pulled the blankets a bit, and that was when he shifted, readjusting the blankets for me.

"Are you cold?" he murmured, pulling the blanket

from around him to allow for me to be able to cover myself up more.

"No, I just..." I was so shocked at being curled up into him, I didn't know what to say.

He sat up, adjusting the covers, and lay back down, pulling me back into him. I'd just gotten comfortable when he wrapped his arms around me and pulled me against him.

I was on my back, blankets wrapped around me, when I woke up, sunlight pouring in through the front window. Tristan was gone and the house was silent. I wondered if I hadn't dreamt the whole thing, and I sat up and ran my fingers through my hair and found a note on the table.

I was careful not to wake you. Breakfast is waiting for you in the kitchen, just needs to be warmed up. I've got things under control at The Biscuit. After I'm done there, I have to run for a meeting with the magazine and then I'll take you to get your Christmas Tree. - T.

I softly smiled, remembering the look Tristan had given me when I'd been talking to Fred. He'd actually listened when I said I didn't have a tree yet.

I grabbed my scooter and rolled my way into the kitchen to find a plate of scrambled eggs and bacon sitting there covered with instructions for heating. I placed the plate in the microwave and followed the instructions while pouring a cup of coffee from the carafe that had been left on the warming plate to keep it hot.

I'd taken my time after I'd eaten and took a hot bath, then dried my hair and got dressed. Then I bundled myself up and made my way over to The Crispy Biscuit. I went in through the front door and stepped inside. All the tables were full. I glanced around and noticed Trinity and Peggy sitting in their usual booth, both ladies waving to me. I waved back and then looked toward the bakery counter. The lineup was long, and I was surprised to see Tristan behind the counter serving up orders. He was smiling and laughing with each customer he interacted with. It was almost as if he'd been in Willow Valley his entire life. Cici was busy waiting on tables, and Melinda was doing the rounds, filling up coffees.

I scooted over to where Trinity and Peggy sat. "Morning, ladies," I said, smiling.

"Brooke! It's so good to see you. How is the foot?" Trinity asked as she moved over, giving me room so I could sit down.

"It's getting there. The scooter helps. I was going to go crazy otherwise."

"Glad to hear that!" Peggy said, smiling. "Things appear to be well here. Tristan is really fitting in."

"Yes," I said, glancing over to the bakery counter and watching Tristan as he carefully packed up another order.

"He's certainly owning up isn't he?" Trinity questioned.

I bit my bottom lip as I watched him smile at Mrs. Cadman, who no doubt had come in for the cookies she always ordered for her ladies knitting group. "That he is," I said, softly smiling at them both.

"Oh my goodness. What is that look?" Trinity questioned, just as Melinda approached the table.

"Brooke! Morning! I didn't see you come in. Did you want a coffee?" she questioned.

I nodded my head and watched as she refilled both Trinity and Peggy's mug then went over to the counter and grabbed one for me.

I looked at Trinity and then to Peggy. "What look?"

"My dear, you like him, don't you?" Peggy questioned, glancing over at Trinity with a knowing look.

"Who?" I pretended as if I didn't know who they were talking about.

"The gorgeous man behind the counter."

I shook my head. "Not a chance. Do you honestly think I could ever like someone who tripped me?"

Both ladies laughed. "Brooke, then you better not look in his direction at all because you're not hiding it very well. I can tell. We've known each other our entire lives." Trinity laughed. "You haven't looked at a man like that since John Longshire, the captain of Willow Valley High's football team, in senior year."

I couldn't help but laugh. "I did have it for him didn't I."

"You did, and I hate to break it to you, but you're looking at Tristan the same way you looked at John, but don't worry, this time the man you're ogling is looking back at you in the same way," Trinity said, nudging my shoulder and laughing.

John had never given me the time of day. In fact, I wasn't even sure he knew I was alive. Trinity was right on that part. I turned and looked over to the counter to see Tristan packing up another order. He lifted his head and met my eyes. He didn't smile, he didn't nod or wave; he just stood there watching me. He passed the box to the customer and then met my eyes again, then he smiled and darted into the kitchen now that the line had cleared up.

"Nah, no way," I said, swallowing hard.

"Well, you can deny it all you want, but seriously, he likes you." Peggy reached over and rubbing the back of my hand.

"All right, you two, enough about this," I said, picking up my coffee and taking a sip. The two women looked at me, and then the three of us laughed.

"So, are you going to be ready for the contest?" Peggy asked, changing the subject.

"I wasn't going to participate after what happened." I shrugged. "Figure that it is somewhat pointless now."

"Oh you have to. The entire town is routing for you!" Trinity said, nodding to the sign in the window.

I looked up and saw the sign announcing the contest that still hung in the window. Somehow, with everything that had gone on, I'd forgotten to tell Melinda to take it down.

"Good luck on the weekend, Brooke," Serenity Johnson said as she walked by our table.

I didn't even have a chance to say anything, she was gone so fast.

Just then Melinda approached the table. "Brooke, can you come into the kitchen for a moment? I need some help."

"Well, ladies, that's my cue. Enjoy the rest of your coffee, and I'll see you soon."

"Oh Thomas will be bringing by the hutch you ordered later today. It's finally finished and honestly, I think, it's one of his best pieces."

"Oh wonderful, I can't wait to see it." I smiled.

"Have a good day, Brooke."

I wheeled my scooter to the kitchen to find it was completely cleaned. Tristan stood there smiling. "What's going on?" I questioned.

"Well, everything is done for today, so, I talked to Melinda and Cici. They said they'd look after everything so we could take off early and go find you that perfect tree," Tristan said, smiling.

I looked around skeptically. There was no way everything was done already.

"It's okay, we'll finish everything up," Melinda and Cici said in unison.

I glanced to Melinda as she smiled and nodded. "Off you go," she said, pushing me gently toward Tristan.

Two hours later, crutches in hand, we pulled into the Willow Valley Christmas Tree lot. "Mindi Potts, she always has the best trees, and she has my favorite type as well—Colorado Spruce!"

"So is that what you want?" Tristan asked, grabbing his gloves from the console.

I nodded, exclaiming, "Yes!" What kind do you normally get?"

"Well..." He cleared his throat. "I don't get one. I'm single, live on my own, and it's not like anyone ever visits." He shrugged.

I looked over at him, suddenly feeling a little sorry for him. Was he all alone, all the time. Where was his family? "So, just because you're alone doesn't mean that you can't celebrate. You could get a fake tree, a small one, just for yourself."

"Ah, it's not a big deal, really. Let's go."

I watched as he got out of the car and made his way around the back to get my crutches out. I couldn't help but notice the sadness in his face. Tristan was really alone, and in my opinion, no one should ever be alone, especially at Christmas.

He helped me out of the car, and once I was steady on my crutches, we slowly made our way over to where the Colorado Spruce trees were, and he began picking up one at a time and bringing it forward for me to see. Almost instantly, I'd found the one I was sure I wanted, but he insisted on looking at more. The more he looked, the more he became like a little kid, picking up one after the other. When I'd disagree, he'd agree with me, and when I would pause and look them over, he would do the same, then he'd pick the one up that I'd pretty much decided on so I could look at it again.

Finally, after an hour, we took the first one I'd wanted over to the binding station. While I waited with the tree, Tristan went over and got each of us a hot chocolate.

"Here you go," he said, handing me my cup.

I smiled and took the steaming cup of hot liquid and took a sip. "Thank you. Did you have fun?"

"I did. This was the first time I've ever done this," he said, looking around at all the other people who were getting their trees, at the kids with large smiles on their faces as they ran around with excitement.

"The first time, like ever?" I asked, trying hard to hide the shock that I was sure lined my face.

"Yep. My parents always had a tree delivered, it wasn't there one moment, but it was there the next."

"Did you at least get to decorate it?" I questioned.

"Nope. Mom had a professional come in, normally while we were in school. However, she always had the most beautiful tree, but it was like a showpiece. Nothing on our tree held any sentiment. They were rented decorations and rented lights."

He grew quiet. His eyes grew glassy, and when I was just about to say something, Mindi's husband, Greg, approached us to get our tree wrapped.

As we made our way over to the car with the wrapped tree, I couldn't help but feel bad that Tristan had never had a Christmas like I had growing up. We stopped at the car. Tristan laid the tree against the side of it and turned to me, taking my crutches from my hands and helping me get into the car.

"Tristan, I was wondering, would you help me decorate the tree tonight?" I questioned.

Tristan nodded. "I'd love to." He smiled, then shut my door.

We left Mindi's lot and drove down the road, coming up to Willow Valley Park. Tristan slowed the car, looking out at the gazebo in the center that was filled with Christmas lights. People were off on the pond, skating around, while some walked and looked at all the additional lights the town had put up.

"Do you feel up for a little walk?" he asked, his eyes still glued to the park.

"Sure," I replied.

Tristan pulled into the first available spot we could find and jumped out of the car to grab my crutches. Then, once again, he helped me to the car.

"It's bound to be a little slippery here," he said, looking down at the packed snow, sliding his booted foot across it. "Yeah, I think it might be best if I hold onto you. Think you can put some pressure on your foot?"

"Maybe a little," I said.

"Okay." He gave me one crutch and took the other back to the car, then placed his arm around my waist, and with me using him for most of my support, we slowly made our way around the park.

When we got to the gazebo, we stopped so I could lean against it and take a rest. He watched as people skated around the pond, and some children off in the distance tobogganed down a hill, their laughter ringing through the air.

"Does Willow Valley set this up every year?" he questioned.

"Every year. They light the large tree in the center of the park in early November. It's quite the event. I provide hot chocolate, coffee, and apple cider, along with a pile of baked goods for everyone, in exchange for a donation to the Willow Valley food assistance program."

Tristan turned his eyes toward me. "You really make an impact on people's lives."

"Nah, it's just something I do. It allows me to give back to everyone who has supported me over the years."

He studied my eyes, then he brought his fingers up and brushed away a strand of hair that had kept falling into my face. "You have an amazing heart, Brooke." He whispered, "I admire that."

Before I knew what was happening, he leaned in and slowly brought his lips to mine.

Tristan

THE DRIVE back was one filled with silence. She hadn't said much after the kiss, and I was beginning to wonder if I hadn't overstepped my bounds. I'd meant what I had said, she was a gorgeous woman with a beautiful heart and a part of me wanted to be surrounded by that forever.

I pulled into the driveway and watched as Brooke hobbled inside, while I untied the tree from the roof of her van. Then I carefully carried it into the house, and together we got it secured into the stand. I placed it in the corner, while she sat on the couch deciding which angle was best. I immediately stopped moving the tree when she shouted that she'd found it. I slowly stepped backwards, my hands out in front of me, in case the thing fell over while she giggled.

"Why are you acting like it's going to attack you?" She laughed.

I shrugged and laughed at myself as I noticed the tree was standing perfectly on its own.

"You don't need to worry, I've never had the tree fall over or attack me once it was in the stand." She laughed.

"That's a relief," I said, continuing to laugh as I looked at her. She really was a gorgeous woman, with the personality to match. "Do you mind if I take a quick shower?"

"No, by all means, go ahead," she said, still admiring the tree in the corner.

When I returned to the living room, I noticed she'd managed to pull boxes marked "tree decorations" out and had most of them sitting against the wall. Except for one box. That box sat in front of her on the floor, and she was going through it.

"What's all that?" I questioned, leaning over the couch and catching a whiff of her perfume.

"Oh, just a few decorations my parents left for me. This one was from my grandmother." She pulled a glass star out from some tissue paper.

I studied her face as she softly smiled as she held it up. "My grandfather gave that to her the first Christmas after she'd opened The Crispy Biscuit because he knew she was going to be a star," Brooke said as she looked at it.

"It's beautiful," I agreed as I looked at the ornament.

Brooke brought her hand up to her eyes and carefully wiped beneath each of them, then she took a deep breath and wrapped the ornament back up into the tissue paper and placed it gently inside the box. "You know, I think I'm going to go and shower before dinner as well."

I nodded, "You're in for a treat tonight," I said, clapping my hands together.

"Oh?"

"Yep, you will see, I'm not spoiling the surprise. Are you okay though? Do you need any help?" I questioned, watching as she grabbed her scooter.

"I should be okay. Thank you though," she said and disappeared into her bedroom, closing the door behind her.

I stood looking at the boxes and then over to the tree that was beginning to fall nicely in the corner. Ever since I'd been a little kid, I'd never really known what a true home felt like. At first, it had made me uncomfortable being here, but now I was beginning to like it. "Don't get to used to it," I mumbled to myself. "You'll be back in your cold apartment before you know it." I glanced to the tree and then turned and made my way into the kitchen.

I'd been working on dinner for twenty-five minutes when I heard the water shut off. I'd just began frying up the breaded chicken, bringing each side to a nice golden brown, and placed it on the baking tray when Brooke came into the kitchen.

"That smells delicious," she said, taking in a deep inhale.

"Chicken Parm, cauliflower rice, and garlic mushrooms for dinner. Sound okay?" I asked, removing the last piece from the pan on the stove.

"Sound okay? You're spoiling me." She laughed and sat down at the table. "Normally, I'd order in pizza or just have a plate of cake or cookies from the bakery."

"If you're going to heal up, you need to eat properly," I replied. "Cake and cookies are not dinner." I smiled. "Even if they are really good."

I put the sauce and cheese on the chicken and sprinkled each piece with a little basil and parsley and slid it into the oven then I fluffed the cauliflower rice and stirred the mushrooms. "Should be ready in about twenty minutes. Can I get you a glass of wine?"

"Please."

I poured the wine into the glasses then carried them over to the small table, placing one down in front of Brooke. "Hope you like it. It's one of my favorites," I said, sitting down across from her and watched while she took a sip.

As soon as the liquid touched her lips, she closed her eyes, savoring the flavor. "This is really good," she whispered.

She slowly opened her eyes and met mine. We sat there

looking at one another, not saying anything for a moment or two, when suddenly, the smell of garlic hit my nose. I jumped up and ran to the stove, quickly stirring the mushrooms. Then I checked the oven; the cheese was melted and bubbling nicely on top, so I pulled the chicken out and quickly plated everything, then headed over to the table with the plates.

After dinner, I'd quickly cleaned the kitchen, then we made our way into the living room where we decorated the tree together. She put on Christmas music, while I did my best to put the lights on the tree, then I lifted her up so she could put the angel on top. Then together we decorated the tree, each of us taking turns placing ornaments on it. We shared wine and laughs, and since I really had no clue what I was doing, every once in a while, she'd take an ornament I'd placed on the tree and move it to a specific location, thinking I wasn't noticing. Soon we were finished, and she turned the lights off in the room and turned the tree on.

The glow from the lights of the tree lit up the room, and we both took a seat on the couch. The tree, the fire, and the music had turned the room into something almost magical, and I looked over at Brooke, who sat there staring up at the tree.

"It looks beautiful," she whispered.

"That it does," I replied in a low voice, meeting her eyes. Only I wasn't talking about the tree. I'd watched Brooke almost all night, and there was something so much more attractive about her than just her looks. The way she took charge of the situation, teaching me every step of the way tonight, never once making fun of me for not knowing how to do something, was so attractive to me. She smiled then turned and met my eyes. Even though we were in dimmed light, I could see a soft-pink hue land on her cheeks.

There by the fire, in front of the twinkling tree, I did something I'd been dying to do since we'd left the park. Ever so slowly, I leaned in and took her full lips with mine. When I felt her hand on my chest, I pulled back and slowly opened my eyes, afraid that she was going to push me away. I actually expected it, but instead, her eyes met mine and then danced down to my lips, then she slowly leaned into me and returned the kiss.

I felt her hand rest on the side of my neck, as a tingle ran through my body. As her lips danced over mine, I ran my tongue through her mouth, and I heard her let out a little moan. My hands traveled to her hip and rested there for a moment before she pushed me back on the couch and straddled my lap.

Her lips came crashing onto mine, her arms resting on my shoulders, as I wrapped mine around her, pulling her a little closer to me, each kiss getting harder and more urgent with each passing second. I could feel myself getting harder with each kiss and knew she could probably feel it as well. I allowed my hands to roam, gently exploring her body, gripping her hips. I gripped the cheeks of her ass, pulling her a little closer. Then she let out a soft moan that sent a wave straight to my cock.

We'd been kissing for only a few seconds, and I could already feel that familiar throbbing sensation I'd get right before I came. I had to slow things down for fear of embarrassing myself. I moved from her lips to her ear, sucking her lobe into my mouth, then I kissed down the side of her neck, nipping and biting as I went. Each time my lips made contact with her skin, she'd let out a soft little whimper, and I knew I was in trouble.

Brooke

MY BODY TREMBLED as he kissed my neck, and my skin pebbled as I felt his fingers dance over the skin of my sides. Every part of my body was awake, screaming for more. He met my lips again, this time taking my mouth hard. His hand wrapped in my hair as he pulled me closer. I could feel his hardened cock, and it was all I could do to stop myself from grinding down on him.

I could feel the heat between my legs and was almost embarrassed by how wet I already was. He released my hair and took a moment to adjust himself, then leaned back on the couch and looked up at me, his eyes full of want. I studied him, then I grabbed the bottom of his shirt, lifting it. He leaned forward and allowed me to remove it. I tossed it behind me and allowed my eyes to wander down his strong chest and abs.

Running my fingers over his chest and up to his shoulders, he was so warm, and he met my lips again. We kissed soft and slow, his hands resting on my hot skin. They went around my back, under my shirt. I allowed his hands to dance over my skin, moving up and down my back. I so badly wanted him to touch my breasts, to run his fingers over my hardened nipples, but he didn't.

When his eyes met mine, I could tell he wanted more. I wanted more. I wasn't sure why he had stopped, so I gripped the bottom of my shirt and pulled it over my head, letting it fall down on the floor behind me. His eyes left mine for only a moment while they traveled to my breasts.

"You're beautiful," he whispered.

I bit my bottom lip and placed my finger under his chin, gently lifting his head to look at me. "Touch me," I whispered.

It seemed to be the push he needed. His fingers traced the top of my bra, my nipples hardening even more. He leaned forward and reached behind me, unhooking my bra, removing it with the lightest of touches.

He stared at my breasts, his hands ever so gently cupping them, then he ran his thumbs over them. I dropped my head back as electricity ran through my body. I thought I was going to explode when he leaned forward and gave a single lick to each nipple. I could hear the sound of my own whimper float through the room.

I reached between us, cupping his hardened cock through his jeans. He hissed as I ran my hand over him. I worked at the button on his jeans, finally getting it open, and was about to very carefully lower his zipper when he stopped me.

"Not here," he murmured.

I didn't say anything. Instead, he held my hand while I got up off him and he stood up. He surprised me by picking me up and carrying me into the bedroom and placing me on the bed.

He stood before me, his eyes roaming my body as he roughly pulled off my pants. Then he bent down, and I closed my eyes, feeling his lips as he placed a kiss right below my navel. Then I heard the clink of his belt as his pants hit the floor, and felt him climb onto the bed, his hands resting on either side of my head. He held his body above me; the only part I could feel of him was his hardened cock pressing into me as he bent and met my lips.

I opened my eyes. The room was still dark, and I stretched. My body ached in places that it hadn't in a long time. I felt lighter than I had in years, and I smiled to myself as I pulled the blankets up around me. Last night had been incredible and I hadn't wanted it to end. I rolled over to see Tristan, sound asleep on his stomach. I didn't want to disturb him, so I carefully climbed out of bed and pulled the door shut behind me, making my way to the kitchen.

Today was the day of the competition, and I sat down with a hot cup of coffee and went over my recipe for my cinnamon buns. As I was reading, my mind kept traveling to what had happened last night. Things between Tristan and I had taken a turn, and they had been for a while now. Tristan was no longer the ass I'd gone to school with. In fact, over the past week, he'd been the one to save my business. I knew, deep down, that without him, I would have had to close for the holidays.

It had been a rocky start, but eventually, he'd cleaned up his act, and in that time, I'd come to know the real him, and I liked what I saw. Something I never could see happening, but he'd changed in the time he'd been here. He'd shared with me over the time he'd been here how unhappy he was at his current job. Although it wouldn't have been hard to tell, since he seemed happier here. Willow Valley seemed to be good for him. He'd made friends in this town, and over the past few days that I'd been back at work I'd noticed that. I'd also noticed that we made a good team. I wasn't sure that he saw it though.

I got up, taking my coffee over to the counter, and began pulling bowls from the cupboard. I had planned on dropping from the contest, but after some thought, it wasn't in me to do that. So, this morning I was going to make these cinnamon buns.

I'd just dumped the flour into the bowl when I heard a noise behind me. I was about to turn around when I felt warm hands slide over my belly and the heat from Tristan's body envelope me from behind.

"Good morning," he said, his voice raspy from sleep. "What are you doing up already?"

I closed my eyes and welcomed the kiss he'd placed on my neck. "Baking for the competition," I murmured, my voice shaky.

"I see. I'd rather hoped you'd still be in bed," he said, his hands traveling under my over-sized shirt. My body was instantly on fire as his fingers danced along my panty line.

"I didn't want to wake you," I whispered, my voice barely audible as I closed my eyes and relished in his touch. "Figured you could use the sleep."

The man had surprised me. I'd never have thought he'd have been this kind of lover. I'd have expected him to be more like he was in his day-to-day life. But he'd surprised me with his tender kisses and gentle touch.

"I see," he whispered between each kiss he'd placed on my neck. "Maybe I'll help you," he said, biting my earlobe.

My body shook. "What...what would the magazine think? You helping the contestant," I said in a low voice.

"Shhhh, no one needs to know." His breath tickled my ear as chills ran through me as his lips met mine.

He rested his hands on my hips and stood behind me. "Let's get these made," he said, taking on a serious tone.

I couldn't help but laugh. "Are you going to stand behind me just like this the entire time?" I questioned.

He gave me a mischievous smile and nodded his head. "Let's go. Can she concentrate enough?" He laughed.

"All right," I said, my cheeks heating.

Soon, I had the dough completely mixed in the bowl and began kneading and rolling it out. Once that was finished, Tristan helped me with the butter and sugar filling, each of us taking turns to cover the dough with it, then I began rolling them up and cutting each one into a perfect-sized bun and placing them in the pan to rise.

I'd just covered it with a cloth and set it on the back of the stove when I turned around. Tristan stood there, the bowl that had held the cinnamon sugar mixture in his hand, watching me.

"What?" I questioned.

"How long will those take to rise?" he asked.

"Probably an hour or so?" I shrugged.

"I see," he said, looking down to the remainder of the contents in the bowl.

I could see that he was thinking of something as he swirled his finger through the leftover butter, cinnamon, and sugar mixture. Then he brought his finger up to his mouth. He didn't say anything. Instead, after he'd licked his finger clean, he swirled it back through the mixture and brought his finger to my lips. When I didn't move, he gently rubbed his finger against my lips, and then brought his mouth to mine, sucking the sweet mixture into his mouth.

"You taste really good." He chuckled, taking my mouth again.

Wrapped in my bathrobe and nothing else, I slid the risen cinnamon buns into the oven while Tristan plated breakfast.

"What time are you heading down to the community center?" I questioned.

"I need to be there about noon. Vicki wants us all there before you guys appear. She said something about needing help with the setup."

I nodded. "That makes sense."

"Come on over and eat," he said as he carried the plates to the table.

I hit the timer and then hobbled over to my seat and sat down, taking a bite of my toast. I watched as Tristan dug into his scrambled eggs and took a bite of the perfectly cooked bacon.

"So, do you have any idea what your plans are after this contest is over?" I asked, a mix of hope and hesitation in my voice.

Tristan shrugged. "Go back to the city, I guess, and continue to eke out some existence with this job."

"If you aren't happy there then why don't you put your talent to use?" I questioned.

Tristan looked up at me, then back down to the food in front of him. "I dunno. I never gave it much thought I guess."

I took in a breath, my stomach in knots as I decided to tell him what I'd been thinking about this morning. "Well, I was thinking..." I paused. Was I only opening myself up to get my heart broken if he didn't like the idea?

Tristan looked up at me and waited for me to begin speaking again. I took a bite of bacon and was just about to start speaking again when we heard a knock on the front door.

"I'll get it." He wiped his face with a napkin and grabbing his T-shirt from the back of the chair and threw it over his head as he made his way to the front door. I could hear nothing but a small murmur, and then he returned.

"Who was that?" I questioned.

"Melinda. She just wanted to pop over and wish you good luck in between serving customers."

I smiled. "That was nice."

"So you were saying..." Tristan said, taking a seat.

"Yes. Well, I've been watching you this past week, and you seem to really like it here."

"Yes, it's a very warm little town."

"Yes, and you've made some friends here."

"I suppose."

"Well, I just thought I'd throw—"

Again, I was interrupted, this time by Tristan's cell phone. "Give me a minute," he said, frowning as he looked at the screen.

"Everything okay?" I questioned, concerned with the look on his face.

He stared at the screen as if something were wrong. "Yep, I just need to take this," he mumbled, and got up and left the kitchen. I heard his deep voice say hello, silence following.

I swirled my fork through the egg yolk on my plate and placed it down on top of the napkin that sat beside my plate, trying hard not to listen to a one-sided conversation. Then I picked up my toast and tore a small piece off, dipping it into the egg yolk and eating it.

I let out a huff and dropped the toast onto the plate and got up from the table, glancing into the living room in time to see Tristan enter my bedroom and close the door behind him. I frowned. I could hear his muffled voice; it sounded important.

I went over to the oven just as the timer went off, and I grabbed the oven mitts and opened the door, a waft of sweet cinnamon and sugar hitting my nose. I pulled the buns from the oven and placed the pan on the cooling rack. They were perfect.

I got busy making the cinnamon drizzle for over top of them and set the bowl aside just as Tristan came into the kitchen, now fully dressed, the phone still in his hand.

"Everything okay?" I asked, swallowing hard.

"Yeah. Great actually. I just got an amazing job offer from a restaurant in LA. I've been applying for years, and finally my ship has come in," he said, glancing at his watch. "Now, what was it you were saying?"

My heart sank at his news. There was no point in continuing that conversation. Besides, I had already lost the nerve of asking him. "Oh it was nothing important," I said, swallowing hard and forcing a smile.

"You're sure? It seemed important."

"No, not at all. It was just something silly."

"Okay, well, I've got to head over and get things set up. See you over there?"

"Yep, I'll be right behind you."

I listened as the front door shut. My body heavy with the fact that I hadn't been brave enough to speak up and tell him my idea overcame me, and a tear slipped from my eye.

The contest was over. The judges had eaten, rated, and sealed their choices. My mind had been preoccupied with the events of this morning, and I had barely been able to read the reactions from the judges. Normally, I was so keyed in, I could tell immediately if I would even place or not. This time I'd just have to wait and see what happened. I'd carefully packed up the rest of my cinnamon buns and placed the container into my bag and made my way out of the community center.

I was just about to make my way to the sidewalk when I heard my name, and I turned to see Peggy. "Brooke, did you want a lift?"

I smiled and waved. "Do you mind?"

"Not at all," Peggy said, making her way over to me and taking the bag from me.

I'd climbed into her car and put my seatbelt on while she loaded my scooter into the trunk before climbing in. "So, just heading back home?"

As much as I wanted to get changed and just relax, I wasn't ready to face Tristan. I shook my head. "Actually, I was going to head on down to Bluebird Books. I wanted to find some new reads."

"All right then, I will drop you off there. I'd come in

and look around myself, but I need to finish up some arrangements for the holidays."

"Thanks, I appreciate it."

"So, how do you think you did? Do we have a new winner?" Peggy asked while backing out of parking spot.

I shrugged. "I'm not sure. I, for some reason, was so distracted I couldn't even begin to tell if they liked my stuff or not." I shrugged.

"Oh, Brooke, you're so modest. I am sure you won." She winked.

"Thanks, Peggy. Would you like the leftover cinnamon buns?" I asked, pulling the container out of my bag.

"Oh, no, I couldn't, but I think perhaps I could take one. It will go nice with my afternoon coffee."

"No problem," I said, pulling out a plastic sandwich bag from my bag and shoving a bun into it. "Here you go." I smiled, placing it in between our seats.

"Thank you. So, tell me, how are things with Tristan?"

"What do you mean?"

"Well, it's not a secret that the two of you like one another. Trinity, Thomas and I saw you the other night at the park," she said, a soft smile on her lips.

I looked out the window as to avoid Peggy's eyes. I wanted to die. Had they seen us kiss? Instead, I shrugged. "There is nothing to tell. He's simply helped me out, that is all," I murmured, thinking to this morning and the tryst in the bedroom that had begun in the kitchen with that sweet, sugary goodness. I'd been so happy to see how happy he was to have been offered a job that I had to let my own happiness go. It was now his chance to shine. He deserved that.

I was about to tell Peggy when she pulled up outside of the bookstore. "There you go, Brooke. I'll get your scooter."

Within minutes, Peggy was gone, and I was snug and warm inside of Bluebird Books. Trinity had gone to pour us a coffee, and I had set the cinnamon buns on the counter for us to have. I busied myself waiting for her, searching through the holiday reads.

"So, I heard that the contest went well. How do you think you did?" Trinity asked, coming out of the small room she used for her coffee room.

"I have no idea. It was hard to tell. So many good recipes this year," I murmured, pulling down one of the newest Christmas releases this year.

"I've heard from some of the ladies in town that Tristan has made quite the impression."

I looked off into the distance, thinking about how everyone at the diner loved him. "That he has." I mumbled, turning my attention back to the stack of books. I just wished everyone would stop asking me about him.

"Brooke, what is it?"

"What's what?" I asked, turning my attention away from the book and looking over at Trinity.

"You're not your usual bubbly self. What's going on?"

"Tristan got an amazing job offer this morning."

"That's fantastic. I bet he is happy."

"Oh it is. I just, um..." My eyes began to burn.

"What is it?" Trinity asked, coming over and taking a seat beside me.

"It's nothing. It's stupid."

Just then the door opened and Thomas walked in. "Hey, Trin, I'm just running over to the hardware store to pick up a few things I'd ordered. Do you need anything from the store at all for dinner?"

I smiled and watched as Trinity shook her head, smiling. "No, but thank you for asking. Drive careful."

Thomas bent down and kissed her. "I'll let you ladies have your coffee. Good to see you, Brooke."

"You too, Thomas."

As soon as the door closed, I broke down into tears. Trinity instantly placed her arm around me, trying to console me. "The news just came at a bad time, I guess. I was going to offer him a job and ask him to stay in Willow Valley. He seemed so happy here, until..."

"Do you love him?"

I nodded my head and wiped my eyes. "I think so."

"Then what's the harm?"

I shrugged my shoulders. "He doesn't feel the same way."

Trinity looked at me, a small smile on her lips. "How do you know that? Have you asked him?"

"No."

"Perhaps you should."

The afternoon passed quietly, and as we sat there talking and sipping our coffee, I began to feel better. Trinity helped me to see that without asking him I had no idea how he felt. When I left Bluebird Books and began to make my way home, I was armed with a plan to ask Tristan to stay in Willow Valley. Only when I returned to the house, my insecurities crept back in as I listened to him talk on the phone to the person I assumed was his new boss and by the time he was finished, I had talked myself out of it.

Tristan

Two Days Later

I PLACED my bags down inside the door of The Crispy Biscuit and watched as Brooke stood behind the counter, a smile on her face as she boxed up the order for one of the ladies from the retirement home.

Since the day of the contest, she had begun acting differently. She'd refused my help at the diner the last two mornings and had busied herself most nights after work. I'd hoped to talk to her the night before last, so she could tell me what was bothering her, but she'd come in after I was already in bed and was gone before I'd woken this morning.

Just as she passed the box over the counter, she caught my gaze. The smile fell off her face. She whispered something to Melinda and took off into the kitchen. Something was wrong, I could feel it. I wandered over to the counter and stood there waiting for Melinda to turn around.

"Hey, Tristan," she said softly, smiling at me.

"Hey. Is Brooke busy?"

Melinda looked over her shoulder toward the kitchen and then back to me. "She's behind on orders this morning and has asked that she not be interrupted."

My heart sank. She'd sat across from me last night, picking at the celebratory dinner I'd made her. Even if she didn't win the contest, she still deserved to celebrate. I'd suggested curling up on the couch afterwards and watching a movie; however, she'd let out a yawn and said she was tired. I'd watched her get up and make her way into her bedroom. I was about to join her when she shut the door behind her, so I'd retired to the couch.

I'd struggled to fall asleep, wondering where things had gone so wrong, and I'd planned to speak with her this morning, but once again, she was gone before I'd woken.

I glanced down to my watch. It was almost ten, and I knew Vicki wasn't going to be late. She'd said she would swing by the diner, so I could follow them out in my vehicle.

"I need to speak with her," I said, making my way toward the kitchen.

"I'm sorry, Tristan, but she really doesn't want to be

bothered," Melinda said, grabbing my arm and stopping me.

I met her eyes and shook my head. My chest hurt, and I had a funny sinking feeling in my stomach. I stepped away, but then turned around and made my way toward the kitchen, pushing the door open. Brooke sat at one of the tables, quietly icing some sugar cookie cutouts, and as the door closed, she looked up. I was about to speak when the door opened and Melinda stepped inside, followed by Cici.

"Sorry, Brooke, I told him," Melinda said, her voice full of irritation.

Brooke met my eyes and put her focus back on decorating the cookies. "It's fine," she murmured.

I looked to both Melinda and Cici who quietly took a step back out of the kitchen, closing the door behind them. I stood there waiting for her to say something, anything, but when she didn't, I took a step toward her.

"Were you not going to say good-bye?" I questioned.

Brooke shook her head, still holding the cookie in her hand, carefully sprinkling white sugar on the white icing. "There isn't anything to say." She shrugged.

"What do you mean, there is nothing to say?"

"Exactly what I said. I already thanked you for helping me with everything this year. Now, you're on to your next big venture, and I already wished you luck with that. What more is there to say?"

"Well, I figured, now that the contest is over, you'd like to tell me what it was you were going to tell me the other morning. You were all words, yet after the interruption, you grew quiet."

"As I told you, it was nothing important," Brooke said, getting up off the stool and moving to grab more icing.

I stood there, not sure what had happened over the last two days, but she wasn't acting herself. I wanted to know what was bothering her.

"Brooke..."

She didn't even acknowledge I had called her name. I was about to approach her when I saw Vicki pull up with Frank, neither of them getting out of the van. I knew she wouldn't wait for long.

"I see the crew is here," she said nodding to the window. "You shouldn't keep them waiting."

"Here is my number. Text me?" I said, placing my card down on the table she was sitting at.

She glanced at me, then down to my card. "You best not make them wait. Good luck with everything, Tristan."

I looked up and met Brooke's eyes. They were red and glassy, as if she'd spent the morning crying. I wanted to wrap her in my arms and was about to step forward when I saw a tremble in her lip. Just then Melinda came flying into the kitchen, pulling a tray of cookies from the rack, and made her way back out to the front. We stood there, frozen, looking at one another, and my heart sank when she turned away from me, bringing her hand up to wipe her cheeks.

"Tristan, your ride is out front," Cici yelled through the door. "They are blocking the fire route."

Not knowing what it was I should do, no matter how much it hurt, I didn't say a word. I turned and made my way out of The Crispy Biscuit. I threw my bags in the back of my car. I was about to climb in when I heard the familiar voice of Fred, the postal carrier, call my name.

"Tristan, my friend, leaving us so soon?" he said, coming around and gripping my shoulder.

"That I am. Heading back to the city," I said, shaking his hand.

"Well, thank you for everything. For keeping young Brooke's dream going. I hope you'll keep in touch. Perhaps come and visit us again soon."

No one had ever said those words to me before. I swallowed hard and nodded. "Sure will. Here is my card," I said, digging into my pocket. "I'd love it if you'd keep in touch."

"Willow Valley is sure going to miss you," Fred said, shoving the card deep in his pocket.

I looked around and realized that I too would miss this small town. It was the first place I'd ever felt welcomed in my entire life. Not to mention, it was the place I was beginning to think I'd finally fallen in love. To say it was going to be easy to drive away was a lie.

"I've got to get going. Make sure you say good-bye to everyone for me. Hopefully, I will see you again one day."

Fred stood back and waited while I climbed into my car. Once I was buckled, I pulled the door shut, and as I pulled away, he lifted his arm and waved. As I pulled out, I stopped the car and went to wave back. It was then that I saw Brooke watching from the window. Tears stained her cheeks as she too lifted her tiny hand and gave a small wave.

I'd been back in the city for three days. In that time, I'd begun packing my apartment and was getting ready to attend my last day of work at *Festive Treasures*. The movers were coming the day after Christmas to take my stuff out to LA where I was going to be the new Executive Chef of Azure.

I left my almost empty desk and walked down the office hall to Vicki's office. I'd sent over my final piece for the holiday issue on The Crispy Biscuit earlier this morning and wanted to get her opinion on it before I wrapped everything up for the day. I approached her semi-closed office door and knocked.

"Hey, Tristan," she said, glancing up from her computer. "Come in."

I pushed the door open and stood just inside the office. "I just wanted to stop in and thank you for everything."

Vicki looked a little confused at my words. I'd never thanked her for anything before. "You all ready to head out in the morning?" she questioned.

"I am. Everything is all packed. My desk is empty."

Vicki nodded. "You know, Tristan, I am sorry to see you go. I know I've always been hard on you, but that was because I knew you were capable of so much more than you put forth. However, you really proved yourself over the past few weeks."

"Why, because the magazine didn't get sued?"

Vicki looked at me and smiled. "Not only because of that. You saved that woman's business, and well, the article you wrote was just...well, it was amazing. You really captured everything. As I read it, well, let's just say I could feel her story in my soul. That piece, well, it's nothing like your other work."

"So, you'll use it?"

"Will I use it? Of course, I will. Honestly, if you were still going to be working here, I would have submitted it to the award committee."

"Really?" I asked, shock lining my voice.

"Tristan, I think it's your best work, honestly. You know, I'd go out on a limb and say that something happened to you in that small town. You changed."

I thought back over the past couple of weeks. Something had happened to me in that small town, something I couldn't explain. I'd thought about it each time I'd sat down to write the article. I'd never deleted, rewrote, deleted, and rewrote more times in my life. Normally, I'd just throw words down, not caring who I impressed or who I hurt, but this story was different. I'd wanted to make sure that Brooke knew that I'd recognized how hard she'd worked to get where she was. I'd also wanted to make her proud, to show her that what we had shared over the last little while had meant something. I also missed her like crazy.

"What do you mean by changed me?" I questioned.

"Well, you're not surrounded by your usual cockiness. You know that your-shit-don't-stink mentality. You've actually turned into someone that I'd wished I'd gotten to know a little better." She softly smiled. "Too be honest, I think that Brooke may have had a little bit to do with that."

"No," I immediately answered, wanting to stomp that idea right out. I'd thought it myself over the past few days. I didn't need someone else pointing it out as well.

Vicki nodded. "Could have fooled me. I mean, the

way you two were looking at each other on contest day, it was like you were two high schoolers in love."

I didn't know what to say to that, and I stood there practically giving my feelings away without even knowing it. "No, I was just simply helping out someone so my boss didn't get sued."

"I don't think you believe that either," Vicki said, clearing her throat. "Do you have any plans until you start at the restaurant in the new year?"

I shook my head. "Thought I'd take my time and drive out there. See some sights on my way."

"Well, you have a safe trip, and if things don't work out, know that you can always contact me."

"Thanks, Vicki, but you don't have to say that."

"No, Tristan, I mean it. If you can produce something as good as you have, then you are always welcome to work here."

"Thanks, Vicki. I'll watch for the publication," I said, tapping the doorframe, then turned and walked away.

"Oh, Tristan?"

I turned around and went back to Vicki's door. "Yeah?"

"This arrived for you this morning," she said, holding an envelope out for me to take.

I frowned and stepped forward to take the bright-red envelope from her hand, flipping it over to see my name neatly written on the front of the envelope. I frowned as I stared down at it. It was writing I recognized almost immediately, and I felt my heart speed up.

"You know, Tristan, I'm sure if you plot out the path correctly, you can always stop into Willow Valley to say good-bye." She winked.

A funny feeling hit my stomach as I nodded, taking what she was saying into consideration. "I'll see you around, Vicki. Happy New Year."

"Happy New Year, Tristan."

I turned, making my way back to my desk to put the last few things into the small box I'd packed.

My apartment was a mess, boxes were everywhere. I'd left what I'd been working on and sat on my mattress. It lay on the floor since I'd dismantled my bed. I leaned back against the cold wall. The small bedside light softly lit the room. My arms rested on my bent knees, and I stared at the small red envelope that Vicki had given me. I still hadn't opened it.

I sat there, twirling it in my fingers, my stomach spinning as I wondered what the contents said. Finally, I got up the nerve, and I tore the corner open. I pulled out the neatly folded piece of paper and opened it.

Dear Tristan,

Don't worry, this isn't instructions, you can breathe a sigh of relief. I hope I didn't take too long to get this to you. I'm hoping you are still at the magazine. If not, hopefully they will forward it to your new address.

It's taken me a while to be able to come to terms with how I was feeling and to be able to write it out. Finally, I did it. First, I really want you to know what your help meant to me. You gave me the best Christmas gift anyone could have given me. The opportunity to keep my business going. It may not seem a big deal, given the fact that I do have staff, but that extra help you offered made the world of difference in their lives. I know I thanked you a million times over. I just don't want you to forget it. That something you did made a difference to someone else.

I also want you to know that I will always treasure our time together. It wasn't too long ago that I never thought your name and those words would leave my mouth in the same sentence. But you changed that too. I miss those nights, even if it were only a couple, that I spent wrapped in your arms. You are a kind and gentle lover, and I am so thankful that I was able to experience that. I may even be a little jealous of the woman who gets to experience that for the rest of her life.

The morning that you got that call, I was planning to ask you to stay here, in Willow Valley. I really felt that you ended up being a great asset to The Crispy Biscuit. I also felt that we had something special. I know you tried to get it out of me, but the reason I didn't say anything was because I didn't want you to give up on your dream. You were excited. The light in your eyes was something I hadn't ever seen in you before. No matter how badly I wanted you to stay, to be near me, with me, I realized on my part I was totally being selfish. How could I, a little girl from Willow Valley, ask you to turn down your ultimate dream. I couldn't. Besides it shocked me when I realized how I felt about you, perhaps scared me a little —well, maybe scared me a lot—and I think that was why I couldn't get it out.

I want you to know I did end up waving good-bye. I did it from the window because I couldn't bring myself to step outside. I also knew if you hugged me one more time, I'd prob-

ably have begged you to stay. I also knew I
would shatter the second you touched me. I
hope that one day I'll be able to see you again.
Until then, please, go forth, live your dreams,
and make yourself a success. I know you have it
in you. You just need to believe it yourself.
 With Love,
 Brooke.

I stared at the letter, the words soon blurring. My heart hurt as the words she had written sunk in. I lay down on the mattress, spreading out, and rolled onto my side, looking at the words again, then I folded it and tucked it under my pillow, and for the first time in my entire life I, Tristan Ryan, cried myself to sleep.

<h1 style="text-align:center">Brooke</h1>

December 23

Tomorrow was Christmas Eve. I'd mailed out that letter to Tristan a few days ago and still hadn't heard anything from him. I was almost certain I'd missed him. I'd just finished loading all the baking trays into the dishwasher and set the machine. My chest felt heavy. I'd figured if he'd gotten it before he'd left that he would at least have written me back or messaged. Yet there had been nothing.

I let out a sigh and sat down behind my small desk in my office, opened up my accounting program, and began sifting and sorting through receipts from this month. I was surprised at how well we had done so far during the month of December. Sales had well blown past what we'd done last year during this time, and they had increased on the Baking Crate site as well.

I'd just gotten everything sorted when I heard a soft knock on the door. "Come in," I called.

Melinda poked her head into my office and smiled. "I'm not interrupting you am I?"

"Of course not," I said, turning my attention to her. "What's up? Everything closed up now?" I questioned.

"Yeah, I just thought I'd bring you the mail before I left," she said, shoving a stack of things at me. "I forgot that Fred dropped it off when he came for the orders."

"Oh just throw it down on the corner of my desk. I'll get to it later," I said, turning my attention back to the mess of receipts on my desk.

Melinda didn't let anything go. Instead, she gave me a funny look and continued to hold onto the pile. "You sure you don't want to look at it now."

"I'm positive. I'm trying to get these receipts sorted," I said, turning my attention back to the task at hand.

"Oh..." Her voice fell and she let out a huff.

"What is it?" I questioned, placing the pile I had almost sorted through down onto the desk then turning to look at her.

"Well, it's just...um...an envelope came from *Festive Treasures*. It's pretty thick."

"It always is. They send out a 'sorry you didn't win' letter, 'but you placed second or third along with a copy of the magazine,'" I muttered. "Just put it down with the others."

Melinda stood there looking at me. I frowned. "Fine, give me the envelope. I'll open it if it makes you happy."

"Yes please." She smiled like a small child and held out the envelope for me to take.

I took it from her and tore at the top of the envelope, pulling out the contents from inside. I barely glanced at the letter. "See, I told you, exactly what they send every single time."

Melinda grabbed the letter. "You didn't even read it! How do you know what it says?"

"Because, Melinda, I never win. I place second or third."

Melinda stood there, her eyes running over the letter as a smile formed on her lips. "You are soo...."

"I'm so what, Melinda?"

"Read it for yourself!" she said, holding the letter out to me.

I grabbed it from her, annoyed that she hadn't given up on this yet, and read the letter.

Dear Brooke,

First, I'd like to thank you for entering this year's Festive Treasures Countdown to Christmas. We were honored to have another returning contestant, and to hold it in your hometown of Willow Valley.

Festive Treasures looks at many things during for this contest. Growth as a baker, growth as a business, and of course the recipe. Over the years, you have grown in all areas. That's why this year I am happy to award you as the winner of this year's Festive Treasures Countdown to Christmas Contest.

Please find included in this envelope a copy of the next issue of Festive Treasures. We will be sending out the plaque along with the twenty thousand dollar grand prize to you in the coming days.

Thank you for being a valued member of our contest family, and we hope you will join us next year.

Sincerely,

Vicki

Festive Treasures Editor in Chief.

I looked up from the letter and met Melinda's eyes. "My God, I...I won," I said, standing up from my desk.

"You did! You deserve it! You've worked so hard," Melinda said, throwing her arms around me.

I sat down on the couch and curled up in a blanket then reached for my glass of wine. I'd come home, gotten changed, and then Melinda and Cici had taken me out for dinner. We'd eaten and celebrated, and then the girls brought me home. I'd come in and gotten changed, turned the fireplace on, put a holiday movie on the television, and had pulled a bottle of wine from the fridge.

I was so happy that I'd won, and as I sat here sipping my wine, something was missing. While my staff was happy for me, and my parents were proud and had congratulated me over the phone, I still had no one to really share my accomplishment with.

I took a sip of my wine and looked down to the magazine that sat on the table. I'd been so excited that I hadn't even looked at the article that they'd written about me yet. I wasn't sure I wanted to. However, I took a sip of my wine and reached for it, opening and flipping through the pages until I found it.

I blew out a breath and reached to turn the small light on that was beside me and sunk down farther in the couch and began to read.

Tucked away in the small town of Willow Valley is

The Crispy Biscuit. A small generational family-owned business. Originally started by Betty and Clarence Higgins, as a small-town diner, Betty's daughter Rita and her husband Fred finally took over the small diner when they were ready to retire. The Crispy Biscuit became a landmark in the small town over the years. It's now owned by Brooke Kinley, the only child of Fred and Rita. Brooke studied at Savory Sensations Cooking Institute where she excelled in all of her courses, especially pastry. Upon returning to Willow Valley, still undecided in her career choice, she seemed a little lost. She never mentioned that to anyone, especially her parents, since they were expecting to keep the small-town diner in the family.

However, over the next two years, devastation hit the Kinley family. Brooke's mother Rita was diagnosed with cancer. This diagnoses that forced them to travel to another town for treatments meant trouble for the small diner. Financial strain was another issue that the family faced as the treatments were not only expensive but they also needed lodging and travel costs.

Brooke watched her parents struggle. Until one night she decided, with her knowledge of pastries, to open up a small counter inside of The Crispy Biscuit and bring to the small town the delicious, sweet treasures she'd learned to make from around the world. She'd hoped to help offset the costs her parents were facing. After all, she'd watched her parents work hard their entire lives to have a retirement they wanted, and now to see them spending it all on health care didn't seem fair.

She worked night and day to make a go of this. Working long hours into the night baking to make sure the counter was full every single morning, she managed to make enough money, with this addition, to support her mother's health care bills.

Over the next couple of years, Brooke ended up getting an account with Baking Crate. Now she can bring her exclusive treats to other parts of the world. Not only was this a building block for her career, it also enabled Brooke to be able to replenish her parents' savings, still helping to support them to this day. While in Willow Valley, I had the opportunity to work with Brooke during this past month. I have never known anyone who puts more effort and care into her business. She cares about each employee, and about the people of her community, and most of the time spends her time doing things to benefit others instead of herself. Not to mention the food, the sweets are all amazing. Willow Valley is lucky to have her, and it's apparent they know it. The support from this small community is amazing.

I urge anyone who is passing through this small town, find and stop in and meet Brooke and her team. You'll not only be greeted with a smile, but you'll be greeted and welcomed into one of the most welcoming towns I've ever been in. Sit down, enjoy a cup of coffee and some breakfast, and don't forget to grab a wonderful treat from the sweets counter. You'll be missing out if you don't.

I stared down at the images that had been included, softly smiling as I saw most of me with my staff, and then I flipped the page to see a large photo of me standing beside Tristan, his arm around me. It was from the night we'd gone to the park after we'd gotten the tree. I'd completely forgotten it had even been taken. We'd stopped in front of the gazebo in the park, and someone from the mayor's office had asked if they could take our picture. Tristan had pulled me into him, and we both smiled as she snapped the picture. I'd forgotten that there would be a copy available for us to pick up the next morning, and we'd never gone to get the photo.

I smiled as I ran my fingers over the image. I picked up

my glass of wine, swirled the contents, and drank down the remains of the glass.

Christmas Eve was one of my busiest days. I was always closed Christmas Day and Boxing Day. I'd started my day early. I had orders for cookie platters, cakes, yule logs, not to mention the place had been packed since we'd opened. Last-minute shoppers bustled in the streets, stopping along the way to get out of the cold and grab a hot coffee and a snack.

I'd just popped the last few trays of cookies into the oven. I'd committed to staying open later than normal today and was quickly running out of baked goods. I looked around. The cakes that were being picked up today were already cooling and would soon need to be decorated. I hobbled over to the mixer and had just starting to make the icing when the phone rang.

"Melinda, can you grab that?" I called as I stood adding icing sugar into the mixing bowl bit by bit.

"Sorry, I'll be there in a couple seconds," she yelled back, running out the door with three trays of cookies stacked on top of each other.

I shut the mixer off and ran over to the phone. "Hello, The Crispy Biscuit," I said breathlessly into the receiver.

"Brooke? Is that you?"

"Dad??"

"Yeah, it's me. How's things?"

"Busy as always. It's not like you to call me at the diner. What's up?" I said, wiping my hands on my apron and sitting down.

The phone went silent.

"Dad?" Something was wrong, I could feel it in the air.

"It's your mom. She had some sort of spell two days ago. I brought her into the hospital and..."

I could hear the shakiness in his voice, the panic. "What is it, Dad? Why didn't you call me?" I asked, panic building in me.

"Um...I don't know how to tell you this, but the cancer it's back, and it's spread."

My stomach sank and my eyes filled with tears as I processed what he'd said. Everything went quiet as I began shutting my surroundings out.

"How bad?" I asked, sitting down trying to catch my breath.

"They aren't sure. They are still waiting on some tests. However, they think it's been back for a while and she just hadn't noticed."

I brought my hand to my mouth to stop the sobs that

so badly wanted to escape. They were in Paris, not supposed to be back until the middle of January. What if she didn't make it? I'd never get to say good-bye. Sobs silently racked my body, but I did my best to compose myself so my father couldn't hear that in my voice.

"What are you going to do? Come home, to her doctors?"

"The doctors here think she is okay to fly, so yes. They will send their findings to her doctor in Florida, and then we will be coming home. I've already booked our flight."

"I want to come see her," I said instantly, forgetting the fact that New Year's was just around the corner and the week after Christmas was a busy one.

"Brooke, what about the diner?"

"I'll be there," I bit out. "Please send me your flight information. I love you both," I said, my voice beginning to betray me.

"Love you too."

I hung up the phone and buried my face into my hands. This wasn't how it was supposed to go, I thought to myself. I looked around the kitchen, my body fully exhausted at the news that had been just handed to me. I just needed to make it through today, I thought.

"Sorry I couldn't get the phone, Brooke," Melinda said, coming in for the second set of already finished trays. She hadn't looked my way, or I knew she'd have stopped and come over to me, and for that I was grateful because I knew I wouldn't be able to keep myself together.

I made my way back into my office, grabbing the schedule off the wall. We were down two staff members per day until after the new year. There was no way I could leave. I glanced at the Baking Crate order cue and noticed a huge increase in online orders for next week. I'd just pinned the schedule back up when I felt my phone vibrate in my pocket. I dug in and pulled it out to see a text from my father letting me know that the doctors weren't going to let her travel.

I dropped my phone on my desk and slammed my door shut. I'd have to go to Paris. I'd also have to close for the remainder of the year, I realized. Most of my staff had family plans, and there was no way I was going to ask them to cancel now. I wasn't going to ruin their holidays because of me. I got up from the chair, wiped my eyes, and went back to work. Focusing on whatever task was in front of me always proved to be my best coping strategy. As soon as the doors were closed, I planned to have a meeting with my staff.

Tristan

December 25

I'D FINALLY FINISHED PACKING, and I sat at the small table in my kitchen. The apartment echoed with every move I made. I cracked open the plastic container that held the rotisserie chicken I'd ordered from the restaurant around the corner and dug my plastic fork into it. I'd spent numerous Christmases alone over the past few years, and it had never bothered me, but this year was different.

I'd thought about trying to call my brother. It had been a few years since we'd last spoken. Every year after Mom and Dad had passed, I'd joined him and his family for the holidays. At the time, it had been more of a pain in the ass to lug my bags over to his house and have his kids crawl all over me with their sticky hands. I still remembered the first Christmas

I'd spent after our falling out. It was a pleasure not to have to get up early. It was also a pleasure to get to finally have a quiet meal. Only now as I sat here, after spending all that time in Willow Valley, surrounded by people, I was actually lonely.

I glanced out the window and looked across into one of the windows in the other building. A family gathered around the dinner table, smiling as they shared conversation and a meal. I looked down to my dinner and shook my head. I truly was all alone.

I glanced down at my watch. My brother would probably just be sitting down to dinner, I thought. I picked up my cell phone and scrolled to his number and dialed. The phone rang and rang, but no one answered. I hung up and stared down at the number. No doubt he was probably ignoring me.

I was about to pick it up again and dial, when it rang.

"Hello," I answered between bites.

"Tristan, Merry Christmas," I heard a familiar voice say.

"Fred?" I questioned.

"Hope I'm not interrupting and that you aren't busy with family, but I wanted to call and let you know I was thinking of you."

I smiled. "Well, Merry Christmas, Fred. How's things out there in Willow Valley?" I asked, hoping he would mention something about Brooke.

"Oh you know, pretty snowy. We got hit with a bad storm a couple days ago."

"Is that so? How's Brooke doing?" I asked, I couldn't wait any longer.

"She's managing."

I frowned. I could only imagine how busy she'd been. Although I was sure she would be closed for today. Yet I didn't like the sound of his voice. It was as if he wanted to say more but wasn't sure he should.

"How's her ankle?"

"Her ankle is getting better every day. She's a stubborn one, you know that."

I chuckled. Fred was right, she was a stubborn one.

"She sure could have used your help, let me tell you. I felt bad for her last night. She was rushing around like a mad woman. Orders weren't ready to be shipped, but don't worry, I made her sit down and take a break," Fred said.

"That's good," I mumbled, thinking back to her letter. Had I been there, this past week wouldn't have been a struggle. "Thank you for caring enough to make her sit down."

"Ah, it was nothing. I just wanted her to stop crying for a few minutes. She was so stressed. I don't think I've ever seen her that bad. Perhaps you could call her. Might lift her spirits a little."

Crying? Why had she been crying, I wondered. "Did you figure out why she was crying?" I questioned.

"She just said something had come up that upset her and she didn't want to talk about it. I didn't want to pry, so I left it alone."

I went quiet, thinking back to her letter. Was she upset I hadn't responded? "I dunno, Fred, I doubt a call from me would help any. We didn't end on the best of terms. Besides, she's probably having Christmas dinner with family."

"Nah, she declined everyone's invite. We invited her, Thomas and Trinity invited her to join them and Peggy, she even had an open invite from Harry and Bessy to come and join them. They put on a big feast for all guests at the inn. She declined everyone."

My heart sank. She really was having a rough time. "Well, perhaps I'll try and call then," I said. "Merry Christmas, Fred."

"Talk to you soon, and have a safe trip out to LA," Fred said. "Make sure you don't forget about us out here in Willow Valley."

I smiled. "That would be impossible."

When I hung up the phone, I thought back to our conversation. I felt that Fred had wanted to tell me something more about the situation, but then perhaps he didn't. I mulled around my quiet apartment for the rest of the night. I decided to get to bed early. It was only eight-thirty. I lay on my back, thinking back to the conversation I'd had with Fred earlier, a nagging feeling in my gut.

I grabbed my phone and looked up Brooke's number. Fuck it, I thought to myself as I stared at the screen. I hit the green call button and waited until it rang. Only she didn't answer, and her voice-mail didn't come on. I hung up and called back, only to receive the same result.

December 26th

Everything had been picked up by the movers and was already on its way. I'd decided to drive instead of fly. I figured I had a couple of weeks before I had to start, and this way I would get to see numerous locations along the way.

I'd stopped for gas before leaving the bed and breakfast I'd decided to stay in for the night and checked my GPS. Luck would have it, there was a lot of construction this way and I'd need to reroute my trip. I studied the map and asked for the shortest distance to get to the next major city and hit start. It started rattling off directions at me faster than I could catch them, and I threw my phone on the console.

I pulled out of the parking spot and began following the course it had picked, left and right, down this side road and that one, until I felt a funny thud. I slowed on the gravel road I was on and slowly pulled my car over to the side of the road, cutting the engine. I climbed out and walked around the car, finally spotting the problem. The driver's side rear tire was flat. I ran my hand through my hair and looked around. I had no idea where I was or how far I was from a service station and the scenery looked the same in both directions. The last place I'd filled up for gas was the last service station I'd seen, and I had no clue how far it was from me now.

I went around to the driver's side and popped the trunk. I had to have my spare. I lifted the floor and noticed that my spare was gone. I'd remembered removing it not that long ago and putting it in storage in the basement of my condo building because I needed extra space in my trunk to bring something home. That spare still sat in the basement of my building. I kicked at the gravel, hating myself for thinking this was a good idea.

When I'd calmed down enough, I looked at my GPS long enough to find the closest intersection, then called my roadside assistance. Within minutes, they had patched me through to an operator and were sending a tow truck.

With the car safely loaded onto the flatbed, I climbed into the front of the truck with the driver. He pulled away and drove slowly down the road, allowing me to take in the vast landscape. He made a turn, and I had to blink twice as I read the words on the sign we'd just past. Willow Valley Retirement Residence.

"I'm taking you to the nearest garage I know out this way. They probably won't have the tire in stock you need, but there is a cute little inn out here that I am sure will have room. It's a quaint little town. Has everything you'll need until they get you up and running again."

"Thanks, I um...I know it..." I said, swallowing hard.

I looked out the window as he drove through town. First, we passed the tree lot on the left-hand side of the road, now empty, a few trees still standing there. Then the park. It was daylight now, but kids skated on the pond, some tobogganing down the hill. I thought back to the first night I'd kissed Brooke by the gazebo and smiled to myself. Then I glanced up and saw The Crispy Biscuit. I'd hoped to catch a glimpse of Brooke, but all the lights were off inside. She must be closed today as well, I thought to myself.

"I'll take you over to the inn, then take your car to the garage. It's not far from the inn."

"Thanks," I muttered, looking over my shoulder in the direction of the small diner.

Two hours later, I'd had an estimated date for when I'd be back on the road. It wasn't as quick as I needed. It was going to take almost two weeks to get the tire, which would make me late for work.

"There's no faster way to get them?" I asked. "I have to be in LA."

"No, no. With the holidays and now New Year's, the distributors aren't shipping. The good news is that they have the tires in stock in the warehouse, but the bad news is they have no drivers until the third of January."

I still had a five-day drive at best to make it out to LA. "Okay, thanks," I mumbled. With my head hung low, I made my way out of the garage and into the parking lot. A gust of wind kicked up, and I pulled my jacket up around my neck. These dress jackets weren't made for this type of weather, I thought to myself. I reached into my pocket and grabbed my phone. I'd have to contact my new boss and let him know I was basically stranded here until after the new year. I quickly hit dial and waited while the phone rang.

"Hello."

"Hey, Lance, it's Tristan."

"Tristan, good to hear from you. Listen, there has been a change of plans. I need you here by the thirtieth."

I closed my eyes. That was in three days. There was no way I could make it. "Ah, Lance, about that..."

"No worries, I've ordered everything for the menu. I

just need a chef to prepare it. Marc came down with the flu."

I didn't say anything. I just listened to Lance breathing on the other end, waiting for my response.

"I don't want you to panic. I know you don't know the menu. I promise after this, you can design whatever it is you want going forward, but for now, we have to go off the old menu."

"That isn't the problem. I was driving out there, and well, I got a flat."

"Ah, so fix it."

"I'm trying. It's just, I'm in a small town, and well, they can't get the tire I need until after New Year's."

The phone went quiet. "Well then get to a bigger town or get on a flight."

"Look, I'm not near an airport. You're going to have to work with me on this. It's sort of out of my control."

Again the line went quiet. I had no idea if he was still there or not. Then I heard him clear his throat. "Tristan, do you want this job?"

"Very much so."

"Then I suggest you do whatever is in your power to get here. Do I make myself clear."

"Lance, you're not being fair. I was on my way out. It's just my hands are tied. My contract date wasn't until after the New Year anyways. You're just going to have to give me a little more time."

"We need someone here who is flexible, Tristan. Things change at the speed of light in this industry. Listen, you let me know what you want to do. I take it if I don't see you here on the thirtieth that you've decided not to take the job and I will move on to the next candidate."

Even at her worst, Vicki had never given me an ultimatum. Irritation lined my body. Everything inside of me screamed that this wasn't what I wanted. I looked up to the sky, then around the small town.

"I'll do my best," I gritted, then hung up the phone.

I pocketed my phone and looked around, wondering what to do next, when I saw the postal truck across the street. The driver's seat was empty, and then I saw Fred walking down the driveway. I looked both ways and made my way over to the truck, leaning up against the driver's side.

Fred had just gotten to the end of the driveway when he looked up and saw me standing there. "It can't be," he said.

"Hey, Fred."

"Tristan, what the hell are you doing here?" he asked, shaking my hand.

"Ah, you know. I was on my way out to LA when I had to take a detour. I was driving down some stone road when I got a flat. The tow truck brought me here."

"That so! Where you staying?"

"Ah, just over at the inn. They said I could check in a

little later this afternoon. I came over to see when I could get a tire. Then I was going to make my way over to see Brooke."

"Ah, I see. So you haven't been over to see her yet?"

I shook my head.

"Well, you won't find her at home," Fred replied.

"Oh? She over at Melinda's?"

"She, um, had to leave town. I was doing a couple last-minute deliveries for her."

"What happened?" I asked, worry lining my voice.

"How about I take you over to Melinda's. It's probably better that she explain it. Hop in," he said, tilting his head toward the passenger's side.

I ran around the truck and climbed up, while he climbed into the driver's side.

I sat in Melinda's small living room and waited while she made us coffee. She carried a tray with two mugs from The Crispy Biscuit along with a plate of cookies and set it down on the small round coffee table in front of us.

"It sure was a surprise to see you at my door," she said, smiling as she sat down and took her mug.

"Well, as I said, I was on my way out to LA and had to take a detour, and voila, flat tire!"

"Will they be able to get it fixed soon?" she questioned.

"Not until after the new year. I guess I'm here until then." I shrugged. "So, Fred was telling me that Brooke is gone away or something."

Melinda nodded her head, a look of sadness lining her face. "Yes, she's closed down the diner until after the new year. It's her mom."

"What happened?" I questioned, lowering my cup, wishing at that moment that I could be there for her, and wrap my arms around her and not let her go.

"The cancer is back. It's not treatable, and the doctors don't think she has much time left. They wouldn't let her leave Paris, so Brooke has flown there."

My heart sank and immediately my mind went to when she told me about her mom the last time. It had upset me to know that she'd dealt with that all on her own, and here she was going through it again.

"She was heartbroken. She did everything she could to help her mom the first time. When I told her we'd manage, she simply shook her head and told me not to worry about it. That it didn't matter," Melinda said, her voice low. "So, I called and canceled everyone's orders for New Year's, and yesterday I went over and posted a note on the front window notifying everyone the place would be closed until further notice. I have no idea when she's coming back."

I looked down at the mug I held in my hand, at the steaming hot coffee, trying to think of something we could do for her.

"I've never seen her so depressed," Melinda said, worry lining her face.

"Did she give a reason as to why she just wanted to close?" I questioned.

"You know Brooke, she didn't want to ruin everyone's holidays. She'd made it so that every employee got to take the time off they wanted to be able to spend with family. She's so selfless that when I looked at the schedule, I noticed she would have been working every day. I offered to take her spot, but again, you know her."

"When does she come back?" I questioned.

"Well, it's supposed to be around the third, unless something changes."

I nodded my head, an idea already populating in my mind. I slowly began to smile. I had a few days here in Willow Valley. I wasn't going anywhere until my car was fixed, and I'd enjoyed working there.

"Melinda?"

"Yeah."

"Do you have the keys to The Crispy Biscuit?"

She nodded, giving me with a curious look.

"Well, I was just thinking. I'm here until after New

Year's. What if we were call all the staff, still go by the schedule she's written, and see if we can't figure it out. We could manage the diner until she returns."

"Geez, Tristan, I don't know. That may piss her off."

I shrugged. "If it pisses her off then I'll take the heat for it. It was my idea."

"Well, I've already canceled all the orders, and even put Baking Crate on hold."

"Do you still have those orders?"

"Of course!" Melinda said, glancing over to the small table where an open book sat beside her laptop.

"I say we undo everything and work together. Get those orders out for Brooke and show her that she too can rely on people."

Melinda looked at me as if I were crazy. Then as the idea floated through her mind, she began to smile. She got up off the couch, grabbed her laptop and her book, and came back over and sat down. Quickly, she passed me the phone, and I began calling the people who had ordered while she reactivated the Baking Crate account and got in touch with the staff.

Brooke

IT WAS ONLY a matter of time. Those words kept running through my head as I sat in the waiting room of the oncology department. This was not the way I'd thought I'd be spending New Year's Eve. In the few days I'd been here, her health had declined, and they were giving her a few days at best.

I swallowed the last little bit of coffee and crunched up the paper cup. My father had needed to take a break from the hospital; he was exhausted, so I'd left him back at the hotel. He hadn't slept, and said he too wasn't feeling well. The last thing I needed was to lose them both, I thought to myself.

I sat there flipping through a magazine. I'd done everything I could to save her the first time, and now there was nothing I could do. It was out of my hands; there was nothing I could try that would save her this time. I put the magazine down and got up and wandered over to the vending machine. I shoved a dollar in and watched as a chocolate bar fell from the dispensing wheel.

I bent down and grabbed the bar, opening the wrapper.

"That doesn't look like a very good breakfast," I heard my father say.

I turned to see him walk into the waiting room and take a seat. I shrugged. "It's better than nothing," I replied and took a seat next to him. "I thought you were going to try and get some rest?"

"Couldn't sleep. I just tossed and turned. How is she?"

"The same. She hasn't woken yet. The doctors say she may not," I whispered, swallowing the lump that sat in my throat. At least I'd gotten a chance to speak with her, I thought to myself.

My father didn't say anything, just nodded.

"Have you eaten anything?" I questioned.

He shook his head, still not saying anything, looking off into the distance.

"Want to head down to the cafeteria?"

He shrugged. "Not that hungry."

He needed to eat, needed to keep his strength up. "Come, Dad, my treat," I said, my voice low. "You need something."

We'd just gotten up and were about to head to the cafeteria when my mom's doctor appeared in the doorway, a sullen look on his face. He didn't need to say anything because we both already knew why he was here.

Mom had passed quietly in her sleep. She'd already been gone a few days, and now Dad and I sat at the airport waiting for our flight. I tried to convince him to return to Willow Valley with me, but he refused. He told me he just wanted to head back home. So, I'd booked his flight to Florida for the same day I was booked to return to Willow Valley.

"You sure you'll be okay?" I questioned, glancing at my watch.

"Brooke, for the hundredth time, I'll be fine," he said, irritated that I was still asking him.

"You can come back with me, you know. Stay for a bit, visit some of your old friends. I know they'd be happy to see you."

"I know I can, and I will come up sometime soon. Until then, I want to get home. I promise I'll be fine. Besides, you'll have a lot to do when you return home. I am sure you'll have to go over everything that happened with The Crispy Biscuit when you get home."

I shook my head. I hadn't told him how I'd been able to fly off to Paris at the last minute because I knew he wouldn't be happy about it. My parents had always taught me that my business should run, even when I couldn't be there. I let out sigh. "About that... I decided it was best to shut it down while I was gone," I mumbled.

Dad looked at me. "Why would you do that?"

"Because, Dad, people had plans for the holidays that I didn't want to ruin because of one of my issues. So, it was just easier to close."

My father looked at me. "Brooke, you do everything for everyone else. Surely, they would have understood."

I shook my head. "It's okay, Dad. I didn't want to burden anyone with anything. I only told Melinda, and I asked her not to mention it to anyone. It was important that my staff were with their families, especially with everything that went on with my ankle. They stepped up for me enough for the few days I was off."

"Oh, Brooke, you're just like your mother," he said, shaking his head.

"Is that a bad thing?" I questioned.

"No, not at all, but you need to learn to rely on others. That's why you have staff, my dear, like I always taught you."

I could feel my eyes burning, and I swallowed hard. I'd

shed so many tears over the last few days, it was hard to believe I had any left. I was about to say something when my father's flight was called over the loud speaker.

"Guess that's my cue," my father said, grabbing his bags.

"Okay, Dad. Safe flight okay," I said, wrapping my arms around him.

He hugged me back, and then I watched as he made his way over to the counter to board. When he was gone, I grabbed my bag and began the walk to my gate.

I'd never been so happy to see the Welcome to Willow Valley sign before. I'd slept most of the flight home, but I was still exhausted. I was looking forward to my own bed and getting back into some sort of a routine. While the cab drove down the road, I leaned back in the seat and looked out the window. We drove by Bluebird Books. I could see Trinity inside at the counter and smiled to myself.

We rounded the corner. The park was full of kids, some skating, some sledding, and I smiled to myself. We came to stoplight, and I glanced over at the post office. I had to do a double take as I saw Fred come walking out the front door with a man who looked just like Tristan. When I turned to look again, the cab pulled away from the curb, and the two men had disappeared around the side of the building.

"Must be more tired than I thought," I muttered to myself as I sat back against the seat.

"Here we are," the driver said as he pulled the cab up to the curb.

I glanced out the window to see the front door to the diner open and a line of people waiting outside. What the hell was going on? I opened the door and stepped out carefully onto the sidewalk, while the driver pulled my bags from the trunk of the car. I reached into my purse and pulled some money from my wallet, handing it to him. "Keep the change," I muttered as I began walking toward the front door.

I stepped into the diner. Cici and Melinda were busy waiting on tables, while a couple of my kitchen staff were working on serving the line at the bakery counter. The diner was full, and I swallowed hard as emotion overcame me.

"Welcome back, Brooke," Bessy whispered in my ear as she and Harry left the restaurant. "Sorry to hear about your mom," Harry said, stopping to give me a quick hug.

Just then the voices in the diner quieted, and I noticed everyone was looking in my direction. Melinda stopped what she was doing and placed the coffee pot down on the counter and smiled.

"What's going on?" I questioned.

"Well, what's it look like? Just another day at The Crispy Biscuit," she said, shrugging her shoulders and smiling. "Welcome home."

She approached me and wrapped her arms around me, hugging me tightly as everyone watched. As I hugged her, I looked over to Cici, who stood with a smile on her face, and to the two kitchen staff who stood behind the counter. Then to all the residents of Willow Valley. Peggy sat over in the corner, tears in her eyes, as she waited for Trinity to arrive I was sure. It was, after all, their day to come in and have coffee together.

Melinda slowly released me, and I looked at her, still shocked at what was before me. "I still don't understand how you did this," I whispered.

"Well, why don't you come on in and I'll tell you." She smiled, wrapping her arm around my shoulders and guiding me to the only empty table in the entire place.

Tristan

I'D JUST RETURNED from dropping off all the Baking Crate orders and had stepped into the back door of The Crispy Biscuit, heat hitting my face. January was colder in this town than December, I thought to myself as I removed my coat and hung it up by the back door.

I went over to one of the cooling racks and pulled a tray of cookies from it. They'd been selling like crazy over the last few days, so Melinda and I had made an extra batch today. I was just about to take it out front when I heard a cheer out in the diner. I smiled to myself. Everyone seemed to be in good spirits today. I lifted the tray and stepped out of the kitchen and froze.

Brooke stood there, in the middle of the diner, a smile on her face. Then she turned and met my eyes. I froze, I didn't know what to say or do. I just stood there, a tray of cookies in my hand, and stared at her.

The diner was so quiet you could hear a pin drop. Cici quickly came over and took the tray from my hands, sliding it onto the counter, then she too stopped.

"Tristan, I..." Brooke went to speak but stopped, tears lining her eyes.

I figured she'd be angry, and I had been right. I'd been the one to overstep, and I'd told the girls not to worry about it, that I'd take the blame.

"Don't be angry at them. This was my idea," I bit out.

"You did this?" she questioned, looking around.

I nodded my head. "I just thought I was helping. Just whatever you do, don't take it out on them. They don't deserve it. Give me a few minutes to grab my things and I'll be on my way," I said, glancing over at Melinda.

She met my eyes and shook her head, trying to signal something, but I wasn't about to be torn apart in front of the entire town. A low murmur broke out in the diner as I backed up into the kitchen. The door had just swung shut when my phone rang. As much as I wanted to get out of here, I knew I had to answer it, so I reached deep into my pocket and pulled it out.

"Tristan," I heard Lance's voice on the other end of the phone.

"Hey, Lance," I replied. I already knew what this call

was about. I was supposed to be in LA today but had decided to stay until Brooke was back.

"So, I decided to go soft on you. You still have a job. I realized I wasn't being very fair to you the other day."

The voices out in the diner were louder now, but I ignored them and concentrated on my phone call.

"So, that being said, your original contract is still in effect. We look forward to seeing you tomorrow for your first day. The staff wanted to know what your plans are for the new menu. I was hoping that you could take some time today and run it over, perhaps go over everything with them."

I began pacing back and forth, running my fingers through my hair. There was no way I could make it out there. Besides, at this point, I wasn't even sure that was what I wanted anymore. I was so focused that I didn't hear the kitchen door open.

"I'm sorry, I can't do that," I responded as I paced back and forth.

I heard him clear his throat on the other end of the line. "I'm sorry?"

"I said, I can't do that. I'm nowhere near LA. You see, I had something come up that I needed to take care of. Something that meant a lot to me."

I took a moment to compose my thoughts as I listened to Lance as he yelled and voiced his disappointment on the other end of the phone. Then, without as much as a single care as to what I was giving up, I simply thanked him for the opportunity and told him my heart lay in a different direction. Then I hung up and pocketed my phone.

With my hands on the wall in front of me, I placed my forehead against the cold wall. It had been the right thing to do, giving up that job, I thought to myself. I closed my eyes, standing there for a moment, thinking about what my next plan of action was. I could always return to *Festive Treasures,* I thought. Vicki had told me that she would look after me.

I was about to push off the wall when I felt a familiar touch as arms wrapped around me. I stood there not moving for a moment, then slowly turned around and saw Brooke standing there with tears in her eyes.

"I'm not mad," she whispered, a tear sliding down her cheek.

"You're not?" I questioned.

"No." She softly smiled. "Quite the opposite. I can't believe you did this for me."

I shrugged. "It wasn't a big deal."

"What about your new job?" she muttered, wiping the tears that had fallen from her eyes. "I take it that was who you were on the phone with?"

I chuckled. "About that...I, um, don't exactly have a new job to go to anymore."

Brooke looked at me, horrified. "Since when? What do you mean?"

"Since a few minutes ago." I shrugged.

"You quit? You didn't even try it out."

I stood there looking at her. I knew what she was thinking, that I hadn't had the confidence in myself to try it out, which was far from the truth.

I nodded. "I did, but it's not for the reason you think," I said, reaching in my jacket pocket and pulling out a folded piece of paper that I held between my fingers.

She glanced to my hand. "What is that?"

I smiled and opened it, looking down at her handwriting. "This is your letter."

"What does my letter have to do with it?" she asked, swallowing hard as her cheeks turned pink.

"A lot, actually. It's the last line you wrote, *go forth, live your dreams, and make yourself a success. I know you have it in you. You just need to believe it yourself,*" I said, reading what she had written.

"Yes, and I meant that, every word of it."

I grew quiet as I folded the letter back up and slid it in my pocket.

"I know you meant it. It also made me realize that the time I'd spent here, they had been the happiest times in my life. I finally knew what it felt like to belong somewhere."

Brooke stood there, listening. She waited while I tried to come up with the words I wanted to share.

"It was solidified when the tow truck brought me here when my car got a flat. Once again, I was welcomed by everyone, Harry and Bessy allowed me to stay at the inn, Fred, Melinda, Cici, all of your customers, everyone was happy to see me. I've never had that type of reception anywhere I've gone." My throat was tight, and I did my best to clear it. "So, over the last week and a half, every night before I went to bed, I pulled out your letter as I struggled to come up with some sort of menu for this restaurant. Yet somehow, no matter how hard I tried, nothing came to me. Then I realized that I was already living my dream. That I was happy, and every morning when I came in here to help Melinda, I felt as light as ever. There was no stress, no anger, no nothing."

"That's wonderful, but it's LA! A high-end restaurant in LA—your dream!"

I shrugged. "Perhaps I had been wrong in thinking that was what I wanted."

"You can't possibly know that. You haven't tried it out yet." She shrugged.

"No, you're right, but that is when I went back to your letter. To the part about how you felt about me."

Her cheeks turned a darker hue of pink and she averted her gaze. "About that. I should have written that," she muttered.

"Why not?"

"I dunno. I don't think—"

I help up my hand, stopping her. "Brooke, I realized that I felt the same way. The time I spent over Christmas, alone, made me realize that I don't want to be alone anymore. You never left my mind. I thought about calling you, asking you to come with me. We'd open a new Crispy Biscuit in LA. Then I realized that if you agreed and we'd gone to LA, there would be no room for you in my life. I'd be working all the time, and that's not how I envision us. I didn't want that."

"You didn't?"

I shook my head. "No, I didn't. I still don't. So I told them that they'd need to find a new chef."

She buried her face into her hands, sobs racking her body.

"I'm sorry about your mom," I said, my voice quiet as I took a step forward and wrapped my arms around her. "I wish I could have been there for you, with you as you went through all that."

When the deep, heavy sobs finally stopped, she whispered, "You were. You just didn't realize it."

She looked up at me with tears staining her cheeks. I placed my finger under her chin and met her lips. I pulled her tight against me as she wrapped her arms around my neck. As our lips parted and she held me tight, I glanced up just in time to see Melinda and Cici watching us from the door. I winked in their direction as they slowly backed out, leaving us. I took that opportunity to kiss Brooke once more, slower this time.

"You want to stay?" she whispered as our lips parted.

"If you'll have me," I whispered back.

"I'll have you." She said, meeting my lips.

Brooke

April

WE'D CHECKED Tristan out of the Willow Valley Inn the afternoon I'd returned and brought his things back to my place. Then we'd called the movers and had them bring everything out to Willow Valley instead. It didn't take us long to get his things moved into my small house, then we donated whatever we didn't need to the less fortunate.

The Crispy Biscuit was busier than it ever had been. Tristan and I worked side-by-side every morning. He'd even taken the time to create some new cookies and baked goods and had added a new breakfast option to our menu.

"Good morning," I murmured as I lay in his arms.

"Morning," he replied, kissing my forehead as he squeezed me closer. "How was last night?"

"Amazing," I whispered.

"Amazing? I don't know if I'd go that far," he said, stretching.

"What? You didn't think it was amazing?"

Tristan looked at me with a teasing smile.

"I wanna do it again. Do you think we could do that again?" I giggled.

He chuckled. "Sure. There is nothing more I'd rather do with you than stay up all night creating some new type of scone."

I couldn't help but laugh. "I'm sure there isn't."

He rolled onto his side, his arm under my head, and looked down into my eyes, his fingers tracing circles around my navel. I pushed his hand away as I giggled. He bent down and met my lips, kissing me deeply.

"We've got to get going."

"In a minute," he said, meeting my lips again, this time his tongue parting my lips as his hands explored my body.

"Tristan." I laughed.

"We have nowhere we have to be," he murmured as he met my lips.

I allowed myself to get lost in his kiss, and soon, he'd kissed his way down my body and now lay with his face buried between my legs. I closed my eyes and arched my back off the bed as he licked and softly sucked at my center, my moans filling the room.

Sunday mornings had become our mornings, each one of them starting out the same way. It was one day during the week that we got to spend together, without anyone around. Afterward, we lazed around in bed, drifting in and out of sleep, until almost nine before we decided to get up. It was almost as if we were making up for lost time.

We'd just sat down at the table when we both heard a knock on the front door. I met his eyes and frowned. "Who could that be?" I questioned, glancing at the clock. It was only nine thirty.

Tristan got up and made his way to the front door, while I sat there quietly and took a bite of bacon. He appeared in the doorway and sat back down, Melinda behind him.

"Morning," I said, pushing out the chair that was beside me for her to sit down on. "Want some coffee?" I questioned.

"No, thank you. I'm sorry to intrude on Sunday, but this really couldn't wait," she said, sitting down.

"It couldn't wait until tomorrow?" I asked. "This must be important."

"It is. Really it is," she said, setting a notepad down on the table.

Tristan and I looked to one another and then back to Melinda. "Well, what is it."

"Well, you know my dad is in the Marines, right?" she began.

"Yes, of course. Is everything okay?" I questioned, worried that perhaps something had happened.

She reached into her notebook and pulled out a single sheet of paper. "He's being deployed."

"I see," I said. I'd known that they hadn't had the best relationship over the years, but since my mom had passed, she had decided to try and work things out with him.

"I'm sorry, honey," I replied.

"Well, you know I've been volunteering my time out at the retirement village, and some of those seniors there are vets. Anyways, one of them mentioned to me that there used to be an army pen pal program. So, I did some research and found this."

I watched as she dug around in the bag she had flung over her shoulder finally producing a sheet of paper that she slid the paper in front of me and I read it over. I looked at her and nodded. "I think this is a fantastic idea."

"Really, you think that people would want to participate?" she questioned.

"I really do. My mom and dad used to hold the pen pal army program years ago. Honestly, I'd be honored to do it again. As a matter of fact, some of the older residents have asked me time and time again why I didn't keep up with it."

Melinda's eyes flooded with relief. "Thank you."

"Well, now wait a moment," Tristan said, standing up and pouring a mug of coffee for Melinda.

"What?" she said, turning and looking in his direction. "Do you not think it's a good idea?"

"No, I think it's an excellent idea. I was just thinking that perhaps you should be in charge of it. What do you think, Brooke?"

I looked back down at the flyer, remembering all the work my mother had done with this, and nodded my head. It wasn't that it would take a ton of my time. My mother had been different. But I could see how much this meant to Melinda. "I agree. I have no problem putting the flyers up, and of course talking to everyone who comes in, and providing coffee and cookies for writing nights like my mother used to do, but I think it's a good idea that you be in charge of it."

Melinda smiled at both of us. "Thank you, guys, it means the world to me."

"Now how about some breakfast?" Tristan said, getting up from his chair and moving to the fridge to pull out more eggs and bacon.

Melinda looked to the both of us and smiled. "If it's not too much trouble? I was so excited I forgot to eat this morning."

"Not at all," Tristan said, quickly getting things started.

As I watched him talking with Melinda while he

cooked breakfast, I realized that I really was head over heels for this man. Once he'd found his true calling and the place he truly felt he belonged, he'd become a totally different man from the one I'd met all those years ago. With each day, I grew prouder of the person he'd become. After all, I knew he had it in him. He just needed to believe in himself.

As Melinda continued telling us more and more about the program, I caught eyes with Tristan. He gave me a wink and mouthed 'I love you.' I felt heat rise to my cheeks. It was the first time he'd said it. I looked down at the table and back up to see he hadn't stopped watching me. 'I love you too,' I mouthed back. He blew me a kiss, and that was when I knew I'd found my forever, and I'd never have thought he would have been Tristan Ryan.

What's Next

Next in the Willow Valley Series is Peggy and Ethan's Story in Letters from the Heart.

I thought I was safe hiding behind a pen and piece of paper. I only joined the pen pal program to appease my friends, so they'd stop bugging me about finding someone new. Then, one afternoon, he appears in my flower shop completely taking my breath away.

Find out what happens in this single dad, pen pal to lovers, thought we'd never meet small town romance.

Available Now

Follow S.L. Sterling

Follow S.L. Sterling

Did you know that bookbub has a feature where you can follow me and it will send you an alert when I release a book or put a title on sale? Sign up here and make sure you stay in the loop.

Bookbub:
https://geni.us/SLSterlingBookbub

Website
https://www.authorslsterling.com

Facebook
https://geni.us/SLSterlingFB

Twitter
https://geni.us/SLSterlingTwitter

Instagram
https://geni.us/SLSterlingInstagram

Tiktok
https://geni.us/slsterlingtiktok

Reader Group
https://geni.us/SapphiresReaderGroup

Goodreads
https://geni.us/SterlingGoodreads

Newsletter
https://geni.us/NLSignupBackMatter

About the Author

USA Today Bestselling Author S.L. Sterling was born and raised in southern Ontario. She now lives in Northern Ontario Canada and is married to her best friend and soul mate and their two dogs.

An avid reader all her life, S.L. Sterling dreamt of becoming an author. She decided to give writing a try after one of her favorite authors launched a course on how to write your novel. This course gave her the push she needed to put pen to paper and her debut novel "It Was Always You" was born.

When S.L. Sterling isn't writing or plotting her next novel she can be found curled up with a cup of coffee, blanket and the newest romance novel from one of her favorite authors.

In her spare time, she enjoys camping, hiking, sunny destinations, spending quality time with family and friends and of course reading.

To be notified of new releases or sales, join S.L. Sterling's private Mailing List.
https://geni.us/NLSignupBackMatter

Get even more of the inside scoop when you join S.L. Sterling's private Facebook group, Sterling's Silver Sapphires: https://geni.us/SapphiresReaderGroup

Other Titles by S.L. Sterling

It Was Always You

On A Silent Night

Bad Company

Back to You this Christmas

Fireside Love

Holiday Wishes

Saviour Boy

The Boy Under the Gazebo

The Greatest Gift

Into the Sunset

Letting You Go

The Spencer Brooks Diaries

Our Little Secret

Our Little Surprise

Our Little Wedding

The Malone Brother Series

A Kiss Beneath the Stars

In Your Arms

His to Hold

Finding Forever with You

Vegas MMA

Dagger

Doctors of Eastport General

Doctor Desire

Doctor Right

All I Want for Christmas (Contemporary Romance Holiday Collection)

Willow Valley

Memories of the Past

To Trust my Heart

Letters from the Heart

What Once Was Broken

Scars on my Heart

The Happy Holidates Series

Pop Tarts and Mistletoe

Champagne and Fireworks

Summer Nights and Fireflies

Vancouver Dominators

Inside the Penalty Box

Ten Minute Misconduct